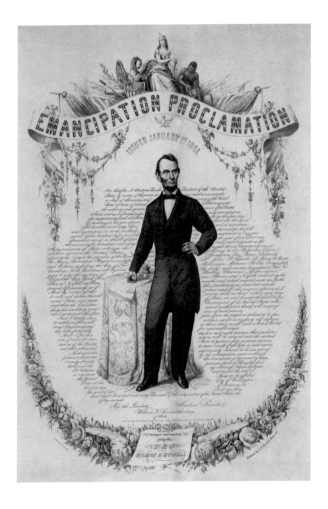

*AUTHENTIC STORM*
*Hearts Touched By Fire, Book 5*
Published by *The Bitter End Publishing*

Copyright © 2021 by Gina Danna

This is a work of fiction.
Printed in the USA.

Cover Design and Interior Format

# AUTHENTIC STORM

HEARTS TOUCHED BY FIRE, BOOK 5

# GINA DANNA

# ACKNOWLEDGEMENTS

This book is Book 5 in the saga of the Fontaines and Silvers families during the American Civil War. The story of Jaquita and Thomas was only made possible by my strong support group who are outstanding, like my editor, Louisa Cornell, who I could not publish without! To JJ Jennings, a dear friend and great research resource for me, especially during this War. To Matt George, who is also another great Civil War research aid and introduced me to the Albany Underground Railway History Education Center and Paul Stewart, who helped on some of the background of the strong abolitionist movement in the area. To my cover designer, Kim Killion, who always makes my books shine! And to my co-workers, who I think now are growing suspicious if they are in the books I write or not, and if so, what they are doing. My muse will never tell!

*"We shall nobly save, or meanly lose, the last best hope on earth."*
~ABRAHAM LINCOLN

*"The American people and the Government at Washington may refuse to recognize it…but…the war now being waged in this land is a war for and against slavery."*
—Frederick Douglass

# PROLOGUE

*West Point Academy
1856*

"This is enough!"

Pierre Fontaine steeled himself. His wife paced the room, her cheeks red with anger and he swore steam spilled from her ears. "Marie, ma chère—"

She stopped, spinning to face him. "No! Do not start! You brought her here and treat her as family, when you know better!"

He sighed, closing his eyes as he pinched the bridge of his nose. "We came for Jacques's graduation, not to bicker."

"Oui, we did. Yet, among our slaves, you hid her. I object that you treat her as anything but help. I have put up with this charade long enough!"

Pierre inhaled. His wife was right and he knew it. Jaquita was more than chattel. He owed her mother more than a life as a slave with a promise for a future that they all knew was probable at best.

"Ma chère," he started again, but Marie would have none of it. She stomped over to him, her eyes blazing. She slapped his cheek so hard it took every ounce of strength he had not to move.

"Mon dieu! Do not return to that old argument that you 'owe' Marguerite anything! She was a house slave you took a fancy to! I had to put up with the humiliation that you bedded her while I recovered up here from losing my mama! And for that, I've had to put up with this child you blatantly claim as yours!"

His cheek smarted and he could tell from the burning sensation that her palm print was blazed on it. Yet he couldn't dismiss her feelings. He had been wrong to do what he did, but he was young, no better than any buck his age. So he let her rage smolder, giving her a moment to recoup and him one to word his response.

"You are correct. My dalliance was poorly timed. Perhaps the loss of you, while I had to remain home to run our plantation, drove me to her. I have apologized numerous times over the years and will continue to do so," he walked up to her, taking her hands in his. He saw the tears forming in her eyes.

"Yet, you must realize, I made a promise—"

"A promise to a slave is not holding!"

"Perhaps." He dropped his tone. "But she nursed me through that bout of yellow fever, the summer before I met you. If it wasn't for Marguerite, I would have died. I told her I was forever in her debt."

Marie glared. "And fathering her child meant you would raise the child with your legitimate children? *Posh!*"

She had broken his hold and stormed to the other side of the chamber. He rolled back on his heels, the throbbing inside his head picking up speed. Always a problem he had up here in the north, during spring, when their flowering trees bloomed.

"And what would you have me do?" He gave up trying to calm her. Giving her ground might solve the issue, or so he hoped.

Marie stopped and turned to face him. "You raised her as an independent child. You had her educated and taught the finer points of life, always dangling the idea she was a Fontaine. You can't 'sell' her at this point and I refuse to continue this ruse any longer. She is of an age to be on her own so release her to do so. And not in Louisiana."

Pierre frowned. "She's barely Jacques's age."

"She's nineteen," Marie virtually snarled. "She is old enough to figure out her way. It is the price you'll pay for your indiscretion."

Pierre mulled the idea. Jaquita was a bright child, even he could see that when she was barely able to walk. She was so cute, with the steel blue/gray eyes always glowing with mischief, though he reckoned she was always processing everything she saw, storing everything away for the future. The problem he found what was the girl's future?

Marguerite had been a house slave since the

moment his father bought her. Lithe and sweet, she'd moved up in the rank, in charge of most but still under their main house slave. As a young man, he couldn't help but be attracted to the light-skinned girl. Their affair, though, was never to be given free rein to continue. He had to marry, and even in French Louisiana, once the land was under the control of the U.S., he couldn't take Marguerite as wife, not for his family's wealth and stature to continue. So he kept her as he married Marie Dupont, a lady he didn't know but whose family held similar rank and prestige as his.

As time flew, and after the birth of his oldest child, Pierre found his attraction to Marie grew deeper but there was still Marguerite. When he was ready to leave his concubine alone, she told him she carried his child. He was doomed. His only way to make up this situation was to raise this love child as his own. And when he let Marguerite go, giving her her freedom in her final days as yellow fever raged over the land, he promised he'd continue to raise Jaquita right and set her free.

Was the age of nineteen old enough to set his child free? His sons, yes, but a daughter's future often meant marriage. There'd be no coming out for his mulatto daughter, hence no suitors of worth in his eyes. He swallowed at what he knew he had to do.

"Yes, ma chère. We will set her free." And God save his soul!

*"We have conquered and occupy the capital of the haughty state that instigated…the treason which has brought on this desolating war…"*

—A Federal soldier under General William T Sherman, February 17 1865 at Columbia, South Carolina

# CHAPTER ONE

*Albany, New York*
*December 1863*

Jaquita McHenry leaned back on the cushions of the carriage, trying to ignore the coolness of the fabric by concentrating on the heat generating out of the foot warmer underneath the soles of her shoes. She had fanned out her silk skirts, hoping nothing was overly close to the small wooden box below with its caged cut-outs, allowing the warmth of the heated brick to be trapped under her petticoat. Winter was dreadfully cold, and no matter how long she lived up here, her Southern heart always craved for home down in Louisiana.

Louisiana. The memories of home hit hard tonight at the Prescott Ball. Seeing her brother Francois, a true Southerner, up here in New York as the war continued had totally shocked her. She couldn't believe what she was seeing. When was the last time she'd seen him, or anyone in the family? Family. That idea made her want to laugh. That 'family' was not only so by blood but also by financial ties…

"Jaquita, darling, are you all right?"

She squinted in the moonlit conveyance to eye her husband as he sat across from her. Thomas McHenry III gave her a quizzical look. She'd almost think he was worried about her—if she let herself.

"I'm fine. Just surprised, that is all." She adjusted her skirt folds absently, silently noting how her white leather gloves gleaned in the moonlight off the canary-yellowed silk with its green and black lacing and ribbons.

Thomas nodded, then reached across and squeezed her left hand. "You're so beautiful."

She gave him a half smile as a reply. That was his standard statement when he was lost as to what to say. She wouldn't razz him for it, because her own emotions were in turmoil. How could the half sister with her darker skin feel when the white family appeared out of no where? Especially here, in New York? And it being Francois, too? How could she explain the whirlwind of memories that involved? And now, of all times?

She stared out the window as they drove down the street, gazing at the town homes and letting the past come to life…

*Summer 1856*

The house in the outskirts of Albany, New York, was an ornate Federalist style house, made of brick and clapboard with Corinthian columns in the front and an upper landing over the front door, outside the doorway on the second floor. Wrought iron shutter locks and adornments decorated the front. It was in every sense a Yankee-styled house with little yardage in the front and not much more in the back, except if the stable with the fenced pasture was counted then the space seemed bigger, though Jaquita still thought this mansion lacked what her home in the South had. She had to shake her head. For now, this was home. She inhaled deeply for a long sigh.

The entire trip north had been a surprise, its ending more so. Jack's graduation at West Point was so grand, it still made her smile, despite the far view that the Fontaine's slaves had. Oh, she wasn't delusional. Her father adored her, like he did her half brothers and sister, but Mrs. Fontaine was tolerant. The woman was never rude to Jaquita and allowed her to be taught by the same tutors her siblings had, though she bet her father pushed that. Yet she definitely learned 'her place' by the mistress very well. Only her father made life in the Big House good.

After her own mother died, when she was a small thing, Aunt Jenny, the slave who ran the house, took her under her wing, teaching her things she knew her white siblings didn't know.

Through Jenny, she learned more about her mother. The Fontaine slaves were civil to her, a very small nod that she was favored by the master, though the depth of their dismissal of her from their ranks took years for her to fathom. Like her mother, many lived here for generations, always slaves.

Yet one thing was perfectly clear the older she got. Jaquita fit into neither world, white or slave, and that proved uncomfortable at times.

As she closed the door behind her, she stared at the staircase before her in the grand foray with the hardwood flooring, striped wallpapered hallway with its large mounted looking glass and side table. It screamed wealth, a richness that clung to everything except her. She shuddered, taking it in that she was alone.

"This is not the doorway for the help!"

The sour voice that boomed down the hallway startled her. Scanning ahead, she saw an elderly man dressed in butler attire barreling towards her with frightening speed. She backed up as he got closer.

"Are ye deaf as well as dumb?" he demanded, now standing in front of her. His dark cheeks were crimson and she swore fire came from his nostrils. She didn't recognize him, but how could she? She hadn't been here since childhood.

"Good afternoon," she replied, tightening her hold on her reticule. "I came with no servants."

The servant snorted. "You humor is ill-placed. If you're to replace that no-good Millie, they must have raked the bottom of the river. You won't last long, making a scene walking in the front door. Hopefully Aunt Lila can make you worth the risk. Take your stuff and head back to her. She is in the kitchen."

Jaquita raised her brows. He thought she was the help and took affront at her coming in the street door. It took her a moment to wrap her thinking around that. As she swallowed the lump in her throat, she couldn't help but realize, after spending her life at Bellefountaine, her father's residence in the South, she rarely went anywhere without someone who shielded her from such assumptions.

"And you are?"

"Clarence, the butler for the Fontaines. Now, you git."

She blinked hard. Clarence wasn't budging until she headed back to see the cook, so she grabbed her satchel that she had dropped and gave the trunk a look. She couldn't haul that but, after getting the situation settled, she'd have it taken to her room. Giving the old man a hard glare, she went toward the back, confusion and anger brewing deep inside.

Her walk to the back of the house took longer than she thought. The mansion didn't look as big as Bellefountaine but appearances were deceiving. What wasn't broad in the front was long in the back. At the end of the hall stood a wall. Faintly, she could hear noises beyond but how would she get there? She'd seen no one else here outside that brutish butler. Infuriated she couldn't find the door or passageway, she put down her bag and crossed her arms, tapping her foot. *This was ridiculous!*

She fumed, staring at the walls and wanting to use those cuss words she'd heard from the field hands and overseer when crops came in. But even alone, she didn't vocalize them because she saw the answer. To the right and left of this back wall was a crevice, not big enough to hold more than a statue or plant, the middle was decorated with an eight-foot tall portrait of her father, Mistress Marie and their dog Louis, a large Irish Wolfhound she'd never seen but had heard stories of. The painting was a distraction of the slit in the crevice that had a small onyx knob. Giving the knob a pull, the hidden doorway swung open to another narrow hallway lit by small windows.

Each step down the hallway brought her closer to the source of the change in the scent. Where the house was clean, the air fresh with a fresh floral tone, back here, the tune changed. The further back she went, the floral disappeared and the smell of roasted beef and all the fixings danced in the air. When she walked into the place, she grinned.

"Aunt Lila?"

The big Black woman working over a large mound of dough on the worktable glanced up, a frown on her face from being interrupted until she saw her. "Jaquita? Child, what a surprise to see you! Come to your favorite aunt!"

Jaquita grinned, dropped her bag and raced over to the cook. "Its so nice to see a friendly face," she moaned, hugging the lady back.

Aunt Lila chuckled. "See you must've run into Clarence. Yessum, he does come across like an ogre." The woman looked down at her, tipping her chin up. "Now, did he make you cry?"

Jaquita bit her bottom lip, trying to wipe the tear that escaped. "No, no. Its just, just," she inhaled. "Its so strange to be here."

"Where's your pappy and the rest? Thought you all left after Massa Jack's graduation."

Jaquita stepped back. "They did. Pappy said it was time I stayed, make my own life."

The cook's face flamed. "He did not!"

She only nodded. "I think he and Mistress Marie got into a row over me. I know she's put up with me, as it were, my whole life. Never mean to me, or anything, just let me know I'm not her child." She shuddered. It'd been a strange relationship with that woman. She was loving to her own children but to Jaquita, she was cool.

"Well, guess it is about time. Those folks always were a bit off, when there's a mulatto child involved."

Jaquita frowned, aggravated. "You make that sound like this is my fault."

The cook rolled back and laughed. "No, child, no. The fault is your pappy's. Now, take it from me, one who knows this family a bit. He was in love with your momma. They were silly over each other. But this sad world would not let that be. No. He had to marry a white lady, one he barely knew but it was agreed it was a good match. Problem was, he couldn't give up your momma. No sir! Made things a bit scratch with him and the missus, that's for sure. Especially when you was comin'. That Miss Marie was nearly fit to be tied! But soon she was carryin' Massa Jack, so all cooled for a bit.

"Now, the problem started when you were a youngin'. Massa Pierre only felt it right to raise you with his white children, learn how to read and write and such. But when your momma fell ill, he worried. Made a promise to her you'd be free." She took Jaquita's hands. "And you is free. Never take that for granted! Its something we all long for."

Jaquita smiled awkwardly and withdrew her hands. She walked around the table Aunt Lila had been pounding dough at, tracing her finger in the flour residue still on it. "I barely remember Mama. But Pappy gave me a locket that has her picture in it. She was pretty."

"Just like you."

"Hmmmm…." She wandered over to the cooling rack near the back window. Grabbing one of the rolls off it, she glanced at Aunt Lila. "So the staff here are still slaves? You're in a free state, and Pappy ain't here." And she bit into the bread before the cook could yell.

But Aunt Lila simply laughed. "Child, if you're hungry, just ask." She walked to the big pot at the fireplace and scooped a ladle of stew out and put it into a bowl. "Here. Eat this with that. Now, don't be shakin' that pretty little head of yours. Take it."

Jaquita took it but managed to squeak out, "You're not answering my question."

Aunt Lila bent over the working table with a knife, running it over the top to collect the flour. "Yes, we're still slaves, in a sense. No freedom papers, but free to do as we please since no one here to order us." She chuckled. "As long as we don't get in the papers, in jail or in the river, or spend all our allowance before the next, then we're left alone, until they come to visit."

"Seems a bit unusual."

"So it seems, but it works. Clarence too busy keeping up with his spit and polish, most the rest hire themselves out after chores. But we all know our place." The cook's face went stone cold as she added, "We're well aware of that law that keeps us in place. We keep the peace and only lack a paper sayin we free, but otherwise, we *are* free." Putting the knife down, she took a cup of lemonade to Jaquita. "And best you act the same before some snake oilman sells you to those catchers."

That comment made Jaquita bite her tongue. The Fugitive Slave Law had slave catchers in the North, looking for runaways and the law said they could send any they found back down South. News spread that sometimes, freedmen were caught, the catchers claiming they were runaways and, with the law in place, those unfortunates could be sent South to slavery. A nightmare that made Jaquita shudder. Despite the tolerance and semi-affection from Louisiana, she'd never been scared. Here, she found herself thrown to the wolves.

*Later that evening*

Clarence was truly rattled after spending the afternoon barely able to contain his edginess. As he rummaged through the house, he found himself at the kitchen door and, after a moment debating with himself, forced himself to go in where he found Aunt Lila, elbow deep in flour.

"Aunt Lila, I declare I always find you here, covered with flour and whatnot." He gave her a crooked grin before he started wandering the room.

The cook gave him a glance as she pounded her dough. "Clarence, dinner was nigh on an hour or so ago. You can't tell me you're hungry."

He shrugged and still continued to look. "We're in a mess, you know." He pulled an apple and bit into it, not even tasting it.

Aunt Lila sighed deeply and shaped her dough, putting it on the board for the oven. "We don't have much choice. We have to make sure Miss Jaquita is a good girl and not get into any trouble, if I understand Massa Fontaine's letter right."

Clarence snorted. "Massa Fontaine. If he wanted that girl so protected, he'd kept her home!"

"Oh, now, Clarence, you saw Missus face when they were here for Massa Jack's graduation. That woman done decide she's tired of watching a slave child that is the favorite."

Clarence finished his morsel and nodded.

"Yessum, I saw her. Definitely looking like she was about to spit blood."

Aunt Lila chuckled. "Probably did, and at him. But he asked and we will."

He leaned forward. "Well, we've got our hands full! She's a spitfire, and pretty. You know what that'll bring."

"She's a Fontaine, clear as day, that is true. None of those children ever quiet longer than a moment. And, just like them, has the looks." She rolled back on her heels, her mouth curling. "Well, all we can do is our best. Though, we best be better than that, keep her out of trouble." She sighed.

Clarence shook his head. They were to keep watch on Jaquita and keep her safe. In New York, he added. "Well, it'd be easier keepin' the devil in hell than keep a ribbon on a girl like her." He downed a cup of water, his insides tight and twisted. How the hell were they going to babysit a Fontaine? Disgusted, he rumbled off, swearing at every step and feeling older than his forty-two years…

*"Here, before God, in the presence of these witnesses, I consecrate my life to the destruction of slavery."*
—John Brown vowed at the Congregational Church, Hudson, Ohio, 1837

# CHAPTER TWO

*Two weeks later*

The rolling carriage stopped in the market place. The driver leapt off the perch with ease and lowered the step out in preparation for her exit. Jaquita pulled her gloves tighter, as if that was possible since they clung to her like a second skin, and took her reticule strings through her fingers right as the door swung open.

"Market place, missy."

She gave the driver a smirk. He stood there, not a tall boy that was sure, but looked smart in his livery. His eyes twinkled with amusement as he gave her his hand to assist. She didn't know this stable boy. And this was the first time in town since her arrival, but when Aunt Lila complained her supplies were low and how she would've sent a boy to market, Jaquita volunteered, claiming fresh air would lift her spirits.

The last two weeks had been quite an eye-opener for her. Clarence eventually came around to respecting her as a free woman and a Fontaine. Most of the help, though sparse, gave her space. Aunt Lila ran the house, leaving her with little to occupy her time other than sleep, ride her horse that her father shipped up, and embroider along with other accepted tasks. Being a lady here was extremely boring.

"Thank you, Alex. I shall return shortly."

The boy's facial expression scrunched with uncertainty but he kept his mouth shut and simply nodded. "Yes, ma'am."

Jaquita chose to ignore that look. Perhaps he was going to say something but what? She refused to let the fear of intimidation that lingered in her head to take control. She was shopping for food. Why would anyone stop her? Running the flat of her palm down the sides of her belled skirt, she inhaled deeply as she could in a corset and steeled herself.

As she walked down the street way, she noticed a few of the passersby glancing at her, a couple of the colored women glaring. It was no different than the house staff had been once Aunt Lila informed them of who she was. It appeared a well-dressed lady with dark skin seemed to be unusual but she knew it wasn't. New York had more freedmen than the South did.

"Now look at that! Thinkin' she's somethin'!" The Irish lilt caught Jaquita's attention and out of the corner of her eye, she saw the two women, dressed in working clothes. Their ire at her outfit amused and irritated her. But with determination in place, she didn't give them a pause and continued to the first stall of greens for sale.

"Whatcha want missy?" the elderly women working the stand stated.

"I'll take five bunches of that, two heads of…" she rattled her order off as she scanned the offerings. The growing season was in full swing, however she missed the abundance home had. Of course, market there wasn't as big either, nor the population as dense.

"That comes to five dollars." The old woman spat on the ground behind the stand.

"Why I never!" she exclaimed. "That's highway robbery!"

The worker shrugged. "You come dressed all fine then complain about how the war be gouging prices ain't no concern of mine. You should git your mistress to stop dressing you like you got it or give you more greenbacks to spend."

Jaquita gasped. "You think I'm a slave?"

The woman squinted at her. "Girl, I don't care what you are. Just pay the money."

But she didn't have that. Her coinage maybe went a tad over a dollar. It hadn't occurred to her she had to pay. "You don't charge the house?"

"This ain't the South, ma'am," she snarled. "New York too bloody big for me to go running to every dang house for money, if you git my meanin'."

Jaquita rolled her lips in, glancing again into her ridicule. This was crazy. Now she needed to get money out of the amount her father sent. At Bellefountaine, business accounts were set up so all the bills were sent. Here? Aunt Lila never told her it was to be paid there.

"Here, Mattie," a male voice behind her announced, his extended hand holding the money, reached to the sales lady.

The old woman snatched the cash and reached over with the basket of produce.

"Pardon me?" Jaquita squeaked, watching the scene as if she wasn't there. Who was this man? And why was he paying for her food? She spun to glance at him. He was tall. She was almost at his chin. He had dark hair, a chiseled face, blue eyes and gave her a dazzling smile that entirely caught her off guard.

He reached past her, took the basket of produce he paid for and offered it to her. "Problem solved."

She frowned as she took the basket, her ability to think escaping her at the moment. "Thank you, I believe, is in order." She stepped out of the way for the next customer. "Who are you?"

"A white knight?" He laughed as he paid for his goods. "Truly no pun intended."

She gave him a half grin at his humor. "Granted. But really, who are you?"

"Thomas C. McHenry the Third." He gave her a bow. "Though I go by Thomas. Never took a liking to Tom."

"And you shop the market early?" She scanned the area. "I don't see many gentlemen dressed like you here." He wore black wool pants with a dark gray frock coat and an emerald green waistcoat gleamed from underneath. Way too dressy for the street market...

"Actually, I was on a run of sorts. Demands from

powers that be made me long for a brief escape and I came for pastries." His grin widened as he leaned closer and added as a whisper, "Sinful, I know, but at times, an indulgence I'll take."

"Well, I must thank you again."

"You are welcome. Now, please excuse me but I must run. So nice to meet you, Miss?" He tilted his head.

"Miss Fontaine."

"Excellent. Have a wonderful day, Miss Fontaine." And in a second, he was gone.

Jaquita rolled back on her heels with a blissful sigh. He was so handsome and so beyond her touch, because he was white…

Thomas couldn't erase the grin on his face, not even when he entered the double doors to McHenry & Phillips offices in the city. The image of that lovely Miss Fontaine danced before his eyes and he found himself quite smitten with her. Her complete surprise at him saving her day was so refreshing. A change from so many of the women he knew, who took it for granted that a man would help them.

"Good morning, Cedric," he greeted his law clerk as he breezed by.

"And you as well, sir," the young Black man replied, standing out of his desk chair, leaving his jacket on the back of his chair. Normally, Thomas would remind him he had to be suited in case a client—or his father—arrived, but today, he let it slide as he slid into his office chair at his desk near the window.

"Sir, your father has already called for you."

Thomas leaned back against the padding on the chair, pinching the bridge of his nose. The window seat he had so badly coveted for years had its downside. When opened, the filthy air of the factories blocks away slowly eked into the room. Add to that the mention of his overbearing father, Thomas struggled to keep his happy attitude.

"I am sure I'll catch him shortly," he replied.

"And Miss Lancaster sent you a note." The clerk handed him the missive.

That woman's name instantly made his smile vanish. Allison Lancaster was a social butterfly, flittering all along New York's rich neighborhoods, friending all she met, but when they turned their back, she was judgmental and gauged each by what they could do for her. Beautiful, she managed to get them to her, but her bite was often fatal, he decided. And he could make that call as she had maneuvered her way into being his fiancée, courtesy of his father.

He took the note and tossed it to the stack of papers on his desk. He did notice how Cedric kept a neutral look at that, which was one of many reasons why he kept this talented young freedman with him.

"Speaking of my father, where is he?"

"Why, son, I am right here," the booming answer replied. His father was standing behind Cedric, having sneaked into the room it appeared without either of them noticing.

"Father, what a pleasant surprise." It wasn't but no point starting the debate he always had with the man. Inside himself, he steeled for the first volley while Cedric slipped out.

Thomas McHenry II took a chair across from his son's desk and leaned back, pulling a cigar out of his pocket with the lighting sticks not far behind. Thomas rolled his eyes. He hated the cigar smoke but his father never listened so he was thankful the window was open and the smell drowned in the factory scents.

"I saw Allison stopped by to see you. Such a lovely girl. You two will have beautiful children."

Thomas's gaze narrowed. "Perhaps."

"Have you set the date?"

"Father, we have not progressed that far," he countered. Ever since this arrangement had been suggested, both his father and Allison had taken it as set in stone they'd marry. Thomas, though, had not.

"There's no time like the present," the man stated as he lit the Lucky Strike and put it on the end of the cigar.

"Father, please," Thomas started. "You know Allison would never take a small ceremony or elope, and with the war, this seems a bit hurried. She'd have a guest list that I'm sure would overwhelm most of the city in chairs and such."

His father grimaced and leaned forward. "It's a good match, Thomas. One your mother and I both agree on."

That made him snort. "Great. Then you marry her."

"I will not take that type of attitude from you."

The tone made Thomas pull back. "I'll retract that statement, sir."

His father's lips twitched as he drummed his fingers along the chair's armrests. "We must come to an understanding. I expect you will make a great statesman and manage this law firm long after I'm gone."

"Why did you not run for office, sir?"

The senior Thomas inhaled. "I had a family to manage. Washington was not in the future for me, but I see it in yours."

"Perhaps. If it helps in abolishing slavery." Thomas stood firmly on that.

"A worthy cause, that is for sure. Just do not close yourself off to those prelates on that. They are a radical group and not worthy of your notice."

Thomas glared at his father. They were both part of the abolitionist movement, members of the Albany Society, though his father did not attend the events after the first one. Instead, he contributed toward it. Thomas, though, definitely participated in all the rallies and attended the lectures, the need to make a change coursing through his veins.

"Instead, dear boy, work on your marriage and your run for office. Then we'll discuss the anti-slavery people." And on that note, the man left, right as Allison appeared at the door with a huge grin on her face.

Thomas bit back a groan as Allison leapt in.

"Good morning Thomas! I happened to be back in the area, so thought I'd stop in and see if you got my message." She sat primly on the chair his father had just vacated, her hands clasped in her lap.

He gave her a hard look. Allison Lancaster was the daughter of his father's best friend, a man who was not only a lawyer but a politician. A Senator in Congress, if Thomas recalled correctly. Allison was his only daughter, well educated for a lady and in fact, just returned from a finishing school in France, his father told him. She was eight years his junior, making her nineteen. She was tall, a wisp of a girl with a waist that rivaled any wasp he'd ever viewed. Her blond hair was coiled on her head in a pinned down masterpiece he was sure, though her bonnet hid the bulk of it. The flowers, ribbon and lace that peeped out of the brim around her face framed her face in the latest in style of fashion. Her green and white striped day dress with her cream-colored shawl also fit for the upper New York business district and its outlying mansions. She'd never worry about lacking funds for shopping, a voice in the back of his head murmured and that made him snort.

She sat patiently, waiting, when he realized she mentioned her message. The note he had tossed aside.

"Good morning, Miss Lancaster. No, I have not had the privilege of reading it."

"Posh, you know me well enough to call my Allison."

He smiled. Of course, she'd jump to intimate form of address. "Miss Lancaster, at this point of the day, priority claims the moment."

She sighed. A flash of anger flared in her eyes but quickly vanished when she smiled again. "Tsk tsk, so it is. I invited you to a soiree I'm hosting next Saturday. I do so hope you can make it."

He leaned back. It was Tuesday and she was on the edge of her seat over an invitation. "I will have to check my calendar, though it sounds delightful."

Her face brightened. "Fantastic! I will see you there! Now I must fly! Tootle-do!" And she was gone.

He sank into his chair. Marriage, shackled to her, would kill him!

*"As for whipping, a slave don't get whipped according to his crime, but according to the ambition of his master."*

—Fugitive slave Lewis Clark reported; Ambition referring to the master's disappointment/realization that his 'perfect slave' was not real.

# CHAPTER THREE

Jaquita adjusted her skirts once she mounted her horse, taking care to cover her knee over the horn of the sidesaddle. It was a nervous task, because she knew it was all positioned right once she was on the stallion. The horse tossed his head and Jaquita patted him.

"I know, Maximus, I know. I'm ready now." She pulled up the reins, getting ready to make a clicking noise to start when another horse walked up next to them, the lead in the hand of the stable boy. It was Alex, the boy who drove her to the market the other day. Startled, she sat, staring at him.

"Mornin' Miss Jaquita. Heard you were fixin' to ride. Thought I'd better bring ole Digby up to join ya." He smiled as he shoved the straw hat back on his head.

She looked at the big white horse with its cropped mane. The horse stared back and that unnerved her a bit, more so because the equine had a blue eye on the right and a brown on the left. Alex chuckled as he pulled the reins over the horse's head and then leaped onto his back.

"Don't worry none about his two eyes. Gives him color in this view, Aunt Lila claims. Mr. Clarence thinks Digby is a devil horse."

"And you?"

He shrugged. "Ah, he's just a horse. We git along fine, so they all leave him to me. But he can git in your face if you let him."

Jaquita bit her lip. "That's not exactly what I meant. Why are you here? I didn't ask for an escort."

"Yessum, ma'am, but Aunt Lila tole me you needed one." The boy shifted in the saddle. "You be in New York and it ain't safe to ride alone, being a lady and all."

With the Fugitive Slave Law, the cook was correct. Jaquita worked hard not to grind her teeth. "Well, I welcome your company Alex."

He smiled broadly. She bet he was hesitant about showing up and how she'd greet him. Surprised was the first thought, but she had to give Aunt Lila credit for watching over her.

They trotted down the street as she scanned for the sign to the First Market Bank and Trust. Her father had told her in his last letter that he placed money in the account for her to use. The street was busy with the wagons and other riders but it didn't take long to get there and she dismounted, handing Alex her reins. Inhaling deeply as she straightened her skirts, she walked in.

Unfortunately, her mood quickly changed by the time she got to the clerk at the window.

"I need to withdraw funds from my account," she announced to the clerk who hadn't looked at her.

Slowly the young man raised his head, adjusting his spectacles. He raised a brow when he asked, "And who sent you for this?"

Confused, Jaquita shot back, "I did. It is my account."

"I see. And you are?"

"Miss Jaquita Fontaine."

The clerk scanned the ledger. "I have a Fontaine by that name. But we don't give money out of a large account to darkies."

Her breath caught. "I beg your pardon?"

His eyes narrowed. "How do I know who you are?"

Jaquita shut her eyes. He wanted a form of identification? Since when? "I fail to see the issue. I am Miss Jaquita Fontaine. I have a letter from my father, if that will suffice." She dug thru her reticule and retrieved it.

The clerk took the letter, the look on his face skeptical. He read it and gave her a glance. "Miss, surely you understand any amount you wish to withdraw is not the type we would allow to persons of your…"

Embarrassment fought with the anger that erupted inside her. "Of my color, I take it you mean." She tapped her foot, getting madder than a hornet. "Well, I's be free, massa, so I don't need your stinkin' money to buy it!" she snapped, mimicking their view on slaves even though her inner self cringed at it. How dare they condemn her like a child! Or, what was the other nasty reference? A chimp? Oh, how she wanted to scream!

The worst was the clerk's demeanor, looking down his nose at her. Add to that the three other customers behind her, two of which she heard whispering while they glared at her and the other just stood, looking bored by the whole affair. It all set Jaquita to a roiling boil.

Instead, it took every ounce of energy she could muster to pull her emotions in. She stood straight yet still managed to snatch the letter back, folding it neatly to put it back in her reticule.

"I shall see what my lawyer has to say about this. Good day, sir!"

Alex stood by the horses, waiting. He realized he spent most of his life 'waiting' to be told what he had to do. For being in a 'free' state, he couldn't help but feel trapped by these pale skinned people. He looked at the horses and found a moment of peace. He knew they didn't worry about what was next. They were tied to a hitching post, though his gave a small toss, a nod as it were, when he stared at the stallion.

Bored. He was bored. How much longer could she be? He had chores to do before he could take his horse for a ride in the fields…

The door to the bank flew open and Jaquita stormed out. Startled, Alex snapped up, grabbing the reins to both horses. She looked mad and he swore he could see fire in her eyes the closer she got.

"We are leaving," she snapped, taking her mount's lead from him.

"Yes, ma'am." As he scrambled to help her mount, she pulled up almost without any aid from him. Made him virtually fall as she slipped out of his cupped hands. His hat fell from his head and he quickly snatched it up right as she turned her horse toward the way out of town. He jumped onto his horse and yanked Digby around to take off after her.

Out of the corner of his eye, he noticed only one person came to see what all the commotion was about. A woman from the bank. And as he rode further away, he thought he caught a glimpse of a smile on her face.

Jaquita trotted home, frustration, aggravation and anger growing. She sat, prim and proper, just as she was taught. Just like her siblings had been instructed. A dry snort came despite her trying to stop it. But she was educated like her brothers and sister. She could read and write and do mathematics, something not normally taught ladies, but her father had insisted. Her education included running a household, riding and all the other means to live. But here, on her own in New York, it was for nothing.

That thought brought her to a halt. She needed to scream, but that was not going to do it. Lifting her knee off the riding hook, she dismounted, spun and started uncinching the saddle.

"Miss Jaquita," Alex said, trotting up behind her and jumping off his horse. "Is somethin' wrong?"

She pulled to loosen the girth and gave a yank to off the saddle. "No, what I need is you to assist me up and then take the saddle back."

With a frown on his face, Alex cupped his hands for her to step into. "Miss Jaquita, I can't leave—"

"You're not being left behind," she replied, picking up the reins and made the horse step back. "I'm just going ahead. Ha!" She heeled her horse and took off, astride her mount, as she raced down the lane. The breeze raced past her, tipping her bonnet back but the ribbon held. The drive toward the house wasn't long like she had in Louisiana, however the greens in the back gave her room to race back. There was a certain sense of freedom that ran through her blood as she had her mount race back and pivot around the back garden hedge, the Arabian bay cutting the corner tight. Astride his backside, her long riding skirt whipping on the left and the skirt on the right trailing upward, she bent forward, keeping a firm yet loose hold on the reins as her bonnet struggled to stay on. Around the turn, Jaquita pulled the ties and let the silk and flowered lace piece whip off her head, yanking a couple hairpins with it. She couldn't contain the laughter, letting the moment steal her ladylike appearance.

Yet as Maximus skidded to a halt as he neared the front steps after rounding the house, Jaquita caught a glimpse of Alex waiting for her with his horse. There was also a carriage there she hadn't seen before. There was company? Aunt Lila stood near the doorway with a frown, Clarence was at the door, stoic, and a white woman next to them gave her a questioning gaze.

As her horse halted, Alex rushed up, taking the dropped reins. "You got company, missy," he whispered.

Biting her lower lip as she tried to keep herself poised but ready, she slid from the horse's back and straightened her skirts as best she could. Steeling herself, she turned. "Good afternoon."

The white lady smiled back. "Miss Fontaine?" At Jaquita's nod, she continued, "Mrs. William Wainwright, nice to meet you."

Jaquita narrowed her vision, hair bristling on her neck. "How may I help you, Mrs. Wainwright?"

The woman, who was probably a head taller than herself, eyed the stallion Alex was walking away. Not only was she tall, but she reeked money, Jaquita decided, all dressed in a striped silk day dress and jewels dangling from her ears, echoed money to spend. Jaquita was willing to bet the woman probably had never ridden a fiery horse like an Arabian nor ridden bareback from the looks she was giving her now.

"Rather small horse, though beautiful."

Jaquita tried her hardest not to snort, but it was difficult. "Arabians tend to be that way."

"Is he yours?"

Now the bristling spread as the visitor judged her. "Yes. A gift from my father."

"Oh. Well, apologies, but I was at the bank

when you were there. I heard that insidious snake deny you access to your money—" she stopped and gave her another judging look. "It is your money, correct?"

Jaquita's neck tensed. "It is."

"Well, perhaps we could help each other."

"And how might that be?" she walked back toward the house and ran into Aunt Lila with her tray of tea. The old servant gave her a brief shake of her head, stopping her from going any further. The cook gave a quick glance upward, reminding Jaquita of her missing bonnet. She quickly smoothed her palm over her plaited and pulled back hair sweep, readjusting a comb that threatened to fall.

"Tea?" she offered, leading her guest into the house, following Aunt Lila's path to the front parlor.

Mrs. Wainwright took an offered seat at the settee. Holding the cup in her hand, she gave a very pleasant smile to Jaquita and started.

"I saw you at the First Market Bank and Trust. What a terrible commotion that clerk started."

Jaquita's brows furrowed as she wondered where this was going.

"I take it, from your accent, you hail from the South." She sipped her tea, never taking her gaze of Jaquita.

"Yes, arrived from Louisiana a few weeks ago."

The woman's brows raised. "Arrived. From the train, as it were?"

Jaquita's cheek twitched. "The train from Chicago, yes. My trip north was not what you are insinuating."

"I hadn't said a word."

"No, but I understand that, considering my color, you might think me one of the many who ran from the South." She stirred her tea absently. "But let me assure you, I am not a runaway."

Mrs. Wainwright nodded. "And your funds. How do you propose to get them?"

"Where, may I ask, are you going with this, Mrs. Wainwright?" The woman was leading somewhere and Jaquita frankly wanted to end this now. Being put on the spot over that rude clerk made her mad.

"Miss Fontaine, please," Mrs. Wainwright said, putting her tea on the side table. "There's someone I'd like you to meet. He could help you with your banking situation, as it were."

That was a twist from what she feared she'd say. "Truly?"

"Yes, you see I am a member of the Albany Anti-Slavery Society. The abolitionist movement is growing stronger, considering all we are hearing from those taking the Underground Railway north to freedom. Speakers like Frederick Douglass and Harriet Jacobs have moved many of us to push for the freedom of your kind." She sat back, with a hint of a smile on her lips. "Several influential New Yorkers are part of the abolitionist movement and one in particular I know, is in a position that could help you with your financial situation."

Jaquita's heart thudded wildly. Writing to her father had been her next alternative, but with the rising concerns of the North versus the South, she wasn't sure how soon he'd be able to help. If she could find another way, she'd jump at it. "I am interested. Please continue."

"Well, the Society meets this evening. I do believe he'll be in attendance. Would you like to join us?"

Settling herself into the chair more comfortably, Jaquita smiled. "That would be delightful."

*"Always mystify, mislead and surprise the enemy…
when you strike and overcome him, never let up in
pursuit…A small army can…destroy a large one…
and repeated victory will make it invincible."*
　—General Thomas 'Stonewall' Jackson

# CHAPTER FOUR

*Thursday night*

Thomas entered Jennings Hall on First Capital Drive in Albany, just minutes before the meeting was to start. He had found himself smothered in cases that had eaten his day. This was his only outlet to relax yet be motivated. The Albany Anti-Slavery Society, he noticed by the throng filling the auditorium, was growing by leaps and bounds. No doubt motivated by the Fugitive Slave Law. It was irritating and he estimated half his work was dealing with this law.

At least here, he could feel the drive to put up with the madness and celebrate those here who had escaped bondage. It was one place he didn't have to deal with his father, who never ventured into this part of town at night, nor Allison, who believed ladies had no right to be so overwhelmed by this. Inwardly, he laughed. Women were just as deep in the cause of freeing the slaves as men.

It was a festive affair in ways. Wine and bourbon always offered and everyone dressed so fine. He went to find one of those drinks as the main thought of Allison drove him to escape her claws. He found a servant carrying a tray from which he could grab a glass. He prayed thanks and took a sip.

When he opened his eyes, he found across the walkway the enchanting angel he'd seen before. The beautiful mulatto he had helped at the market. *What was her name?*

"Mr. McHenry!"

He shook his head and found the caller near his side. Larissa Wainwright. She was a powerful force in the movement, her husband Duane along with her. He smiled.

"Good evening, Mrs. Wainwright."

She returned his grin. "Always a pleasure to see you. Your help against this dreadful law has been a Godsend."

He snorted. "I do the best I can, considering." He leaned back. "Though I haven't won them all."

"Pish-posh. I have the best of words not all are lost." She winked and it made him raise a brow. "I'm so glad you are here. I have a lovely lady to introduce to you," she continued.

Instantly, the hairs on the back of his neck bristled. "Mrs. Wainwright, I am already—" A dreaded thread of despair raced through him at the thought of Allison.

"She is in need of your attorney skills, Thomas." She laughed. "Let me introduce her."

The doorman banged the metal triangle to get everyone's attention. "Please adjourn to the auditorium. The meeting is to start."

Thomas looked to his right but Larissa was gone. He waited for a moment but as the crowd pushed toward the meeting, he found himself swept up in them. He'd have to meet the girl later. He swore, though, if this was over a trivial legal issue, he'd not be happy. As if he had any spare time to give to Mrs. Wainwright because she asked.

Settling into his seat, he was set to refuse her.

Jaquita fussed with her dress, working hard not to pull on the ribbon that dangled off her hair, mixed in with the looping twist of hair sculpted to give her a polished look. She'd never dressed this fine in her whole life, except for a portrait her father had made of her—one without Missus Fontaine knowing. When he sent her north, he had given her a new wardrobe, full of gowns she'd never wear, because how often did freedwomen go out all gussied up? Or to formal balls? She grinded her teeth. Until tonight. Now she had an opportunity, at an evening gathering of intellectual people and money, all to stop slavery. She couldn't help but be worried, fretful something was out of place or just plain wrong.

The speaker came to the podium, a Black man who ranted on about the sins of slavery and the slavers. She squinted at the tale of the owners for their abuse with the whip or rape. The last made her squirm slightly. Another part of her wanted to scream. To lump all Southerners as violent towards the slaves made her father look bad. And that was a situation she had to wrangle with. Though now they gave her another reason to reassess her home and she didn't like it.

"What do you think of our group?"

She spun at the whisper in her ear and found Mrs. Wainwright at her side. *When had she sat down?*

Collecting her thoughts, Jaquita inhaled. "It is definitely a voracious assembly. I had no idea."

The woman laughed. "Yes, for a first time, hearing Mr. Johnson speak is rather motivating and intimating." She leaned closer. "He lived in the South in his youth. The scene revolted him and he moved North, the cause to free the slaves a life calling."

She looked at the woman, surprised anyone would care that much and opened her mouth to say that when the room broke into applause for the speech. It shocked her, just like the basket that was given to her, filled with coins.

"Donations for the cause," Mrs. Wainwright murmured. "Here. Considering all, let me take that from you."

As the basket was gently taken, Jaquita cheeks heated with a blush of embarrassment. She hadn't given it a thought they'd ask for donations. Between the talk and this, she wanted to leave. Clutching her reticule tighter, she turned to thank her hostess and scram from the room except she found herself in a circle of mixed races, all pressing forward.

"Good evening, I'm so glad you…"

"Hello!'

"Mrs. Wainwright, you brought a guest."

"Good evening, Miss?"

"Ladies and gentlemen, please," Mrs. Wainwright cajoled with a smile, stepping closer to Jaquita, almost like a shield against the storm. "Miss Fontaine, I am sure, would love to make your acquaintance, though you have descended on her like vultures. Mr. Johnson, please, have a word."

Jeremiah Johnson snorted as he stepped forward. Jaquita blinked. The main speaker stared into her eyes, his dancing with a gleam as he stood there, in his fancy clothes. Made her wonder how a former slave, light enough he could mimic a white person in a pinch, could afford such an outfit. Then she laughed inwardly. He no doubt thought the same about her, though her skin wasn't as pale.

"Miss Fontaine," he started. "Please excuse the excitement. We have a tendency to swarm over new attendees as if they might be angels from up high. Please accept my apologies for the mob." He took her gloved hand and kissed it.

She gave him a tight grin, not deciding if he was sincere or jesting. However he meant it, the crowd adored his attention to her from the sighs and claps she heard.

Glancing up from her hand, he winked at her. That slightly irritated her, so she yanked her hand away. "I'm so glad you came tonight."

"It was," she started. "Not an evening like I would have normally planned."

"No, I'd bet not. Here, if you'll take my arm, I'll get you out of this mess." He offered her his bent arm.

Placing her palm on it, she queried, "And to where would you take me?"

He laughed. "The doorway, if it is your pleasure to leave."

"Indeed, it is."

"This way, then."

The path was hard, with him stopping periodically to introduce her. "Where do you hale from, my dear?"

She swallowed hard. "Louisiana."

He stopped and turned. "You do say? New York is a trek from there."

How was she to tell him she stayed here often with her family? That many Southerners stayed in the North during the summer if they could afford it. "I had an invitation, so I came." Invitation wasn't the right word, but he'd never know.

He gave her a sly grin.

As they slid through the crowd, she noticed a young man over to the side, slinging his hat back on and turning toward them. It was the man who'd helped her in the market. She lost her breath when his gaze locked on her. Then she stumbled on her step. Jeremiah caught her.

"Miss Fontaine, are you all right?"

Flustered, she swallowed hard and tried to refocus, though when she saw the man take a step in her direction, her steeled resolve started to crumble.

"I'll be fine. Please, can we continue?" She knew she sounded desperate but she needed to move.

Jeremiah started when the man caught up to them.

"Miss Fontaine?"

She swallowed the lump in her throat. Thomas McHenry, she recalled his name. He was handsome, standing there all in fine black wool frock and trousers, his waistcoat a turquoise blue and the shirt pristine white. He was still so debonair, with his hair pomaded back, his blue eyes sparkling under the candlelight. She couldn't help when her heart puttered at a quickened pace thanks to him.

Forcing a smile on her face, she turned. "Why, Mr. McHenry, what a pleasure to see you."

He took her hand and kissed the backside of it. Made her wish they were not gloved, and that realization made her struggle not to swoon. The sly smile he gave her as he pulled away from her hand virtually mesmerized her, making the slight tension of Jeremiah's arm hardly noticed.

"Mr. Johnson, a striking lecture." His quick acknowledgement of her escort shook her out of her infatuation and added to admiration of him even more.

Jeremiah nodded. "Thank you, sir. To hear from one of our major patrons is so rewarding."

She raised her brows in surprise. So McHenry wasn't only handsome, he had the wealth to support abolition. Made her like him just that much more….

"Posh. A man of your speaking style will go far, as will the movement."

"Again, thank you. Now, if you'll excuse us, Miss Fontaine has urgent business—"

*Urgent, huh?* She blinked. If nothing else, she suspected Jeremiah didn't like the attention McHenry gave him, or more likely, from the look on his face, her.

"Ah, yes. Apologies. Again, wonderful talk and," he turned to her with a slight wink. "'tis great to see you again."

As the man walked away, leaving her speechless, Jeremiah started them for the door. One thing was for sure. His speaking to them now had all eyes focused on her. She squirmed.

*"[I]f we are to die, let us die like men."*
—Maj. Gen. Patrick Cleburne, C.S.A.

# CHAPTER FIVE

Jaquita pushed the needle through the fabric and right into her thumb—for the third time in the last hour. The pain seared into the delicate tissue and with a yelp, she threw the fabric, needle and thread across the room. Suckling on her wound, she stood, shaking her skirt out and glared at the piece she'd been working on. Tatting. Tatting a pillow case. It was a task a lady would do to bide her time. She growled. It was what a *white* lady would do, to keep her hands busy, so the devil wouldn't use them. *Fiddlesticks!*

She picked up her work and in doing so, got a dot of blood on the fabric. That made her growl, putting it down and started to pace. Here she sat, at the Fontaine residence, following the rules that had been driven home on how ladies should act but now, what good was that, other than a way to waste time? She wasn't white. No one here would view her as a 'proper' lady, requiring her to act as one. Each step made her madder and madder until finally, she found herself at the window, staring outside at the backyard. The sun called to her, as did the earth. There, being outside, might bring her the peace that she desperately needed as being 'freed' and in New York wasn't what she expected.

She skidded to a halt. Just what had she expected? Searching for an answer only resulted in one—to act as a lady of the Fontaine dynasty. The mere suggestion of that made her laugh out loud. Those ladies, her 'sister' and 'mother' were white. No one, not even in French Louisiana, gave a colored lady a second thought.

The hint that she was less of a person because of her skin color made her blood boil. Grabbing the first object she saw, she hurled the ceramic figurine at the wall. It broke into a million pieces with sharp edges and that, somehow, took the edge off her anger. Yet the pieces made her realize she better scoot before Clarence came.

She raced out of the parlor and headed toward the staircase. Flying up the stairs, a rush of excitement flooded her. Into her room, she pulled the trunk open and found the working dresses she'd thrown in were still there. At the time she left Bellefountaine, she wondered why Fanny had her pack those but, perhaps, the house slave knew her better than she did. In a flurry, she shed the morning dress with its layers of petticoats and crinoline and replaced them with her corded petticoat, the worn over petticoat and a calico working dress. She sighed as she buttoned the bodice. The comfort of this dress seeped into her bones. Changing into a pair of older boots, she exhaled with renewed excitement and headed outside.

The back lot to the house stretched back as a somewhat narrow yard, way too close to the neighbors. Made her want to laugh, considering home...with a deep sigh, she got to the garden and stopped. The ground was rich and black, the scent like deep dark coffee, alluring and beckoning.

The young maid working in the ground glanced at her with a quizzical look on her face. It made Jaquita giggle as she sank to the ground, running her fingers through the tilled earth.

"I guess you haven't seen many people come and just enjoy the feel of the soil." She grinned broadly.

The girl looked puzzled. "No, Mistress, not around here."

"And who are you? Not sure that I've seen you before."

"I'm Shelly. Related to Aunt Lila. She gets me a few jobs to do, tide me over a bit." The girl swiped at her nose, her dirty hand leaving a mark of soil on the bridge of it.

"Well, Miss Shelly, I'm Jaquita Fontaine. Nice to meetcha." She wanted to offer her hand but knew better. "What are you planting?"

"Oh, just some lilies and such. Aunt Lila likes to make the house pretty."

Trying to pool the now filthy skirt so she could move, she reached out. "Here. Hand me that bucket and I'll help."

"No!" the girl squealed, pulling upright. "Aunt Lila rather particular about who does her planting."

"I think she'll let me. I may be new to the house, but from where I come from, tilling the soil runs in my blood." She smiled.

Shelly still peered at her funny but passed her the bucket. Jaquita wanted to laugh but didn't. Digging her bare hands into the earth, she relaxed, finally feeling at home.

Larissa Wainwright tugged on her gloves as she readied to go knock on the door to the Fontaine mansion. She had spent all night contemplating how she could approach the young lady here and finally drew a conclusion to arrive at her door, during morning visiting hours. She glanced at her companion.

"Mrs. Douge, I'm so pleased you could accompany me today. I think this lady will be a grand help to the movement."

Susan Douge looked out at the tall house front with a critical gaze. "You say she is a freedwoman. From Louisiana?"

"Well, the Fontaines are from Louisiana. I have met Mr. Fontaine once, years back at a lawn party. They are French, perhaps the reason for Miss Fontaine's status."

Susan nodded her head. Larissa couldn't tell if that made Albany's abolitionist queen pleased or what.

"You say they denied her at the bank?"

"Yes, yes they did. I witnessed it and she handled it admirably. Her character, I think, will add greatly to the cause." Now they had to convince her, Larissa failed to add.

"If she's freed, perhaps she will have nothing to do with us," Susan argued, disembarking the carriage.

"Or, perhaps if we help her in the banking issue, she might return the favor."

"Perhaps." Susan's tone sounded vague.

Larissa straightened her shoulders. She had sent word to the lawyer about the situation and had yet had a reply. But she knew Thomas well. Surely he'd help. Confidence flooded her and with each step up to the main door, her determination that this visit was successful won.

The butler opened the door before they got there and it surprised her.

"Is Miss Fontaine home?"

The elder Black man stood back to allow them room to enter. When she pulled her card from her reticule for him, she said, "Please inform her Mrs. Wainwright and Mrs. Douge of Albany are here to see her."

But before he moved, a young boy entered, wearing livery of the stable. The butler stopped him.

"Alex, have you seen Miss Jaquita?"

The boy nodded. "Yessum. Out in the garden."

"Ah, yes. Would you escort these ladies to her?"

The boy's eyes widened. "Yes sir."

As the boy led them through to the back of the house, Larissa's curiosity grew, as well as her concern. The woman said she was freed, yet they were now in the servants' quarters. Puzzled, she opened her mouth right as the boy led them to the back doorway.

"Miss Jaquita right out there." He pointed out to the garden. "Miss Jaquita! Ya got company!"

Larissa expected she'd be sitting, enjoying tea perhaps, but she wasn't ready for what she was doing. Even Susan gasped.

"Now, Miss Jaquita, I understand you're a might upset over the situation," Aunt Lila started. "But these are calling hours. Ladies don't take those hours to dirty themselves in servant chores."

Jaquita pulled the stick out of the earth and slid the lavender plant into the slot and gently filled in the remains of the hole with the loose soil. Rolling back on her bent legs, she wiped the perspiration off her forehead as she looked up at the cook.

"Thank you, Aunt Lila. I appreciate your concern. But I assure you, I'm expecting no callers. And I have no one to call on, therefore," she pushed the locks of hair that had freed itself from her hairpin back into place. "I have my time."

"Yes, but surely you have other, more ladylike, duties you could indulge in," the cook prodded.

Jaquita gave her a half smile. The old woman looked so exasperated that she was digging in the earth over planning a tea that Jaquita wasn't sure if she should apologize for not following some innate rules that white women followed, or should laugh at the thought.

"I was embroidering this morning," she admitted, bending back over the earth. "But why? Its mind-numbing work. Pretty, yes, but to what good?"

Aunt Lila frowned. "It's more fitting—"

"For Mrs. Fontaine, or Miss Cerisa Fontaine," she interrupted. "But for the mulatto half sister at best, not required."

"Miss Jaquita! Ya got company!"

"Oh, my," Aunt Lila moaned.

Jaquita looked up at the doorway to the rear veranda and found Mrs. Wainwright and a Black lady, both dressed in fine day dresses, fanning themselves in the summer heat. Biting her inner lip, she put the stick down and got up slowly, flattening her skirt with dirty hands as she stood. She bet she was a sight for them, hatless, in a calico work dress with mud stains. She swallowed deeply.

"Good morning ladies, I wasn't expecting a soul."

Mrs. Wainwright had a mixed expression, as if she disapproved but not completely. The other lady's brow rose quizzically.

"Please excuse us. I just wanted to the take the chance to introduce you to Mrs. Douge. She and her husband are quite the movers and shakers in Albany's Anti-Slavery Society."

"Nice to meet you, Miss?" Mrs. Douge cocked her head.

"Fontaine. Jaquita Fontaine, from Louisiana. Nice to meet you, Mrs. Douge. What a pleasant surprise." She smiled. "To what do I owe this honor?"

"I thought you two ladies might have a lot in common," Mrs. Wainwright stated. "Mrs. Douge wanted to meet the newest member to our community. I had taken the liberties to tell her I believe your arrival from the Deep South will add to the cause."

Jaquita frowned. "I do hail from down South, though my experience might be not as motivating as you believe."

Mrs. Douge tilted her head. "May I ask, why you are out here, tilling the soil, as it were?"

Wiping her dirty palms on her skirt again, Jaquita snorted. "Well, I had been all prim and proper, embroidering pillow cases, but that was hardly fulfilling. I was—" how was she going to explain how anxious that had made her? All cooped up, acting a role she was hardly comfortable with?

"Distracted?" the guest offered.

Jaquita instantly relaxed, as if this woman, this Black woman, understood somehow. "Yes, you could say that. Seemed rather mundane. After all, who would see them? But flowers and working in the soil, feeling the earth shifting through your fingers is so fulfilling. Therefore, I changed and came out here, throwing myself into it. And the flowers…" She inhaled deeply, a slow grin forming. "Smell so lovely."

Mrs. Douge nodded while Mrs. Wainwright's lips thinned, as if the answer surprised her.

"Yes, I'm sure they will. A left over from days in the field?"

Jaquita blinked hard. "As a field hand?" The

thought made her anger flare. Did she look like a field hand?

"Hardly, Miss Fontaine," Mrs. Wainwright quickly responded, interceding between the two women. "Obviously you learned gardening somewhere."

With a hard stare at them, Jaquita gave them a half nod. "True. I did. From Fanny, our house head slave." She smiled. "She drummed the art of plants into us all."

Neither Mrs. Wainwright or Mrs. Douge returned the grin. Jaquita struggled not to react to that, or the fact that they were making her uncomfortable, like she was a slave.

Mrs. Wainwright shot a glance to her companion. Whatever the message was, Jaquita couldn't tell but the shift in their complexions was undeniable. They were through here.

"Miss Fontaine, thank you for receiving us. We apologize for taking your time. We were not aware that you were not receiving guests now. Perhaps another time would be better?"

Jaquita wanted to growl. They decided her attire and what she was doing scaled her acceptability down. *How dare they!*

"Miss Jaquita," Mrs. Wainwright started. "I did want to share that we may have a solution to your bank situation."

That snapped her out of scowling. "You do? I would be most pleased to hear it."

"We know a lawyer who has had some experience in helping freedmen in situations similar to yours. Of dealing with companies that deem it necessary to keep us in our place," Mrs. Douge stated. "If you would like, Mrs. Wainwright knows him better than I and, I'm sure, would gladly make an appointment for you two to meet."

Biting her bottom lip as she rubbed her dirty palms on her apron again. Jaquita nodded. "Yes, please. I would appreciate it."

"It would be my pleasure. I'll send word when I can arrange it." Mrs. Wainwright was all smiles.

"Thank you."

"Til then, it was nice to meet you," Mrs. Douge said. "Good day."

Jaquita watched the ladies leave. Slowly she glanced down at her hands. They were filthy. Somehow these two women had managed to make her feel beneath them and that, she could not take. With a brief call to Clarence to have a bath sent to her room, she hurried in. All thoughts of tilling the soil fled from her mind.

*"…Whatever may be the result of the contest I foresee that the country will have to pass through a terrible ordeal, a necessary expiation for our national sins…"*

—Robert E. Lee wrote in a farewell note to a northern friend when he accepted command of the Army of Virginia on April 23, 1861, upon Virginia's secession.

# CHAPTER SIX

Jeremiah stopped at the door and took a moment to check that his necktie was in place, his lapels laid right and that his frock coat was straight. Checking the edges of his hat brim, he inhaled. He was ready so he lifted his hand to knock when the door swung open. There stood the Black butler, an elderly fellow with the tips of his hair whitened. The reflection of his eyes told Jeremiah he'd better behave or else.

"Good afternoon. I am Jeremiah Johnson, here to see Miss Fontaine."

The butler said nothing but opened the door wider for him to enter. As the butler sauntered off to tell her he was here, Jeremiah couldn't help the hitch in his heartbeat as his nerves started to frazzle. He frowned. This wasn't the first time he'd called on a lady, so why was he so nervous? The most she could say was no…he shook the thought. He knew he was nervous because she was beautiful and alluring and a Southern transplant who intrigued him. The dress she wore last night was of higher quality than most who lived here. Her manners were superb, as if she'd been raised white. *What was her story?* And it was that question that had driven him here.

"Mr. Johnson?"

He glanced up at the staircase and found the lady there, standing in the middle on her descent down. Dressed in a blue and gold striped day gown, she floated down the stairs and took his breath away. In fact, it took him a moment to realize she had questioned him. He gave her a lopsided smile.

"Yes, my lady. Jeremiah, please."

Off the stairs and walking toward him, she grinned. "Sir, you escorted me out of an event, not off to see my father, therefore, Mr. Johnson, I shall remain formal."

His hand covered his heart as he claimed, "You wound me so!"

She laughed and the sound warmed his heart. This beautiful woman, with her sparkling hazel eyes and blushing cheeks, had an air around her that he couldn't define. It was like she was born to wealth and privilege without the discrimination that followed, and he relished in her confidence. It'd taken him years to grapple with the thought of defining his own life.

"To what do I owe this visit?"

He snapped back to reality. "I have come to invite you on a tour of the Remington Art Gallery."

"It's rather early, is it not?" And on cue, the grandfather clock chimed eleven.

"It's the perfect hour," he replied and offered her his arm.

With a nod, she took it and called the butler for her wrap.

The ride to the gallery was short, for which he was forever thankful. Finding himself in close quarters with her made him nervous and addicted to her all at once. He shifted to try to keep his jitters down and hoped he didn't look like an idiot.

Remington Gallery sat on 54th Street. A grand building, three stories high, it held displays of art from all over the world, yet it remained quaint enough that a small gathering of visitors never felt overwhelmed. It looked abandoned at the moment, to which he sighed relief.

Jaquita peered out the window. "It looks closed."

He smiled, to which she frowned. "Have no worries," he reassured her as he jumped out of the carriage and offered her his gloved hand.

Still with a tight, closed expression, she took his hand and then allowed him to escort her around the side of the building, to the tight roadway. A yell from an oncoming wagon driver made Jeremiah snake his arm around her waist and pull her closer to the building as the conveyance whizzed by. Once safe, he released her, hoping she didn't feel his tension at the close call.

"Whatever are we doing here, sir?" It was a growl that surprised him. "We walked right past the door!"

He inhaled. "The hall does not open for a couple of hours, but, if we go through here, we can get in for a private showing."

She raised her brows. "Really?"

He nodded as he knocked on the door.

It opened and a Black man peeked out the opening. "Oh, Jeremiah, I was wonderin' if you were comin' or not."

As the door swung open, Jeremiah directed her inside. "Now, Isiah, I'm only running a might late. Thank you, though, for helping."

"Anything for the cause," the man replied with a broad grin as he shut the door behind them. "Missus," he gave her a slight bow. Jeremiah couldn't help but grin as she blushed and counted himself lucky to have her with him.

"Mr. Jeremiah, now, don't need to remind ya, but watch your time."

"Don't worry Isiah. We'll be through before you know it."

As they walked to the main hall, near the front, his beauty turned to him, a questioning glare on his face.

"If you have connections to get us in for a private showing," she started. "Why are we being asked to leave—before it opens officially?"

Jeremiah gulped. What a sheltered life she had led, which made him want to the laugh at the irony of that thought since she came from the slavery South. No point dancing around on this, he decided.

"Because, Miss Fontaine, Blacks, freed or not, are not allowed in here except as servants."

She gasped.

Jaquita swallowed her shock as her escort steered her through the exhibits. She vaguely looked at the lovely paintings and statues, hearing him mumble about each piece as her thoughts scrambled. She'd never run across this at home, or not that she recalled. Though a voice in the back of her head countered that she rarely went anywhere and when she did, it was in the presence of the Fontaines themselves. As to that, she'd be seen as one of their servants. Racing through her memories, she searched for comparison and realized, if this status was there, would they have stopped her without Jack or Cerisa or Francois being with her?

But as the time dwindled to a close, Jeremiah picked up the speed of their tour and aimed them toward the back door.

"Wait." She stopped, bringing him to a halt. "So we have to also leave by the back door? Like unwanted guests?"

He rolled back on his heels. "My dear Miss Fontaine, part of our mission at the Anti-Slavery Society is to not only to free us from the bonds of slavery, but to get recognition for the people we are, with the same wants, needs and desires of the white people. And as more of us come to the free states, the more the locals encourage us, yet work to regulate us to minor roles of servants and laborers, not a person with own decisions and abilities to do more."

She mulled his thought and added, "Therefore, according to them, art and niceties like that would be too complicated for us?"

"Yes, for the works of art like we just saw," he growled.

His arm tightened under her palm and she noticed his jawline locked tight. She'd never considered what he was arguing since at home, she'd never seen it. Truly puzzled, she decided it was a question she'd look at later. With her stomach feeling empty and his mood deteriorated, she sought to redirect his thoughts.

"I am hungry."

He stopped and blinked hard. "You're hungry."

"Yes. Let us stop for a bite to eat," she prodded. "I saw a lovely place up the street when we drove up."

"Ah, yes. The Fallen Swan." He gave her a half grin and covered her hand on his arm with his other hand. "Shall we?"

The rounded the corner and walked half the block when the statue of a swan appeared.

"Now, let me—"

But she climbed the steps to the front door, making his voice falter as he raced up to her side. By then she was at the door.

The doorman didn't move and continued to look straight ahead. "Servant's door is in the back."

"Oh, Alfred, you don't really think I should

go there," she wooed with her Southern accent rolling on each syllable.

The doorman, Alfred, glanced at her and in that instant, his dire attitude fled, replaced by a warm smile. "Miss Jaquita, apologies. So good to see you! And the rest of the family?"

She laughed. "They are detained. Only me and my friend, Mr. Johnson."

Alfred shot Jeremiah a quick glance and Jaquita caught a flash in his eyes, over what she couldn't imagine. But he returned his attention back to her and said quietly, "This way."

He led them back to a table on the side. The restaurant wasn't crowded but there were several empty tables around them. "Enjoy your meal, my lady."

"Thank you, Alfred." She sat and the waiter pushed her chair in then disappeared.

Jeremiah took his seat and frowned. "You've been here before?"

"Yes. A couple of times. It is my father's favorite for a quick bite, so to speak." She opened the menu, right as her stomach growled.

"Well, they might not serve you today."

That made her tear her gaze off the selections and look at him above the menu edge. "Really? And why might that be?"

"Because we are colored."

"Oh, please. We're here to spend money."

"Jaquita, you don't have your family with you now," he stated in a low tone. "And your company is an abolitionist."

She snorted. "As I recall, New York is a free state,

with plenty of freed Blacks here. Why would this place, and any others, reject good money from any hand? Dollars from a white hand is the same as from a Black." His assumption that their race defined them badly was starting to irritate her.

"It shouldn't, but—"

The waitress walked up. Jaquita noticed she looked surly at them and that made her frown. The woman stood next to their table, stern and the tension was thick. Jaquita waited for her to say something but the waitress didn't.

"Hello," Jaquita started.

The white woman's chin shifted up. "I ain't used to serving your type. Freedmen are not to be out here. Albert is gonna git in trouble lettin' you all back here."

Jaquita inhaled deep. She'd never had issues like this before. "Annie, right? It's been a while, but I was here just a month or so ago with my family. The Fontaines? Of Louisiana?"

The woman looked down her nose at her with her eyebrows furrowing. "Yeah, I 'member ya. But you ain't suppose to be out here, not wit the likes of him!"

Shocked, Jaquita looked at Jeremiah, who sat perfectly still, and then at Annie. "He's my guest. You should treat him as you would me."

The woman waggled her lips, swallowing hard. "If this git me in trouble, serving the likes of you, you gonna git me my job back?"

Jaquita sat speechless. All she could do was nod. She knew her father had money and most of the people who knew them up North knew he was a planter with means. Though she'd never asked a favor as it were, she hoped she didn't have to.

As the waitress took their order and scurried off, Jaquita realized her hunger was gone and anger sat in its place.

*"Lincoln may bring his 75,000 troops against us. We fight for our homes, our fathers and mothers, our wives, brothers, sisters, sons and daughters!"*

—Confederate Vice President Andrew Stephens, July 1861.

# CHAPTER SEVEN

Larissa Wainwright tugged her blue leather gloves on, replaying again the conversation she'd had yesterday with Susan Douge. The fiery abolitionist, with the quiet façade, had been hard to persuade when it came to Jaquita Fontaine.

*"I realize, Larissa, that you believe she would fit the cause, but I sincerely have my doubts," Susan argued as she arranged the school room for the freedmen's children she taught. "She acts as if slavery is an illusion, from her reactions that day."*

*"Posh!" Larissa handed her another set of slateboards. "She's just arrived. She knows no one to speak of, apparently only traveling north with her father and his children. Its very apparent he's protected her from the realms of reality for the colored community."*

*Susan stopped and faced her friend. "From slavery."*

*"Yes, assuredly."*

*"I doubt that is true," Susan said, picking up where she'd stopped. "Perhaps he raised her with his children,*

not a rarity in a wealthy slaveholder's house. The fact that they did not turn her out with the rest of the slave children is unusual, but then again, maybe not."

"How do you mean?"

Susan gave her a half-smile with a sympathetic look. "I fear the girl has seen many things that she simply refuses to accept." Turning again to grab grammar books, a rather poor set Larissa noticed, but for freedmen schools, so typical. "I have met this type before Larissa. Give her time. If you truly believe that she has the drive and abilities to help forge our movement further, than she'll need to come to grips with her past. Maybe tomorrow or in two months. And something to trigger it, I suspect from the others I have seen, though none of those came from large plantation houses where the size alone can hide evil easier."

"Well, then I shall pray revelation comes quickly," Larissa said. "Because I have seen the makings of a strong woman in her. That episode at the bank demonstrated clearly that she's not afraid of a fight."

Susan hummed as she cleaned the slate board behind the teacher's desk. "Did you ever help her get that problem resolved?"

Larissa rolled back in the chair and huffed. "I haven't made it to Thomas's yet."

"You realize he might be too tied up in litigation to help? Plus he's soon to announce his engagement."

She laughed. "How did you learn of that?"

Susan shrugged. "How I've learned things over the years. By listening. Even up here, in New York, people act as if freedmen are nothing more than fixtures like furniture, unless you need us to do something. Then, all the sudden, we are people."

*"You make us sound despicable."* She shivered.

*"No, just another type of student we need to enlighten."* The Albany abolitionist smiled.

Larissa snorted at the memory and tried to make note of the rebuke so as not to fall prey to it.

The carriage door came open and she stepped out. She had a mission. Help pull the lovely Miss Fontaine over to the abolitionist cause and the first step was to get her access to her money. By the time she got to Thomas McHenry III's desk, she was fired up, ready to enlist him in the cause.

"Mrs. Wainwright, what a pleasant surprise," Thomas said, glancing up from his work, wearing only his shirtsleeves. Embarrassed, he gave her a smile as he shrugged his frock coat back on, pulled the perched glasses off his nose and stood.

"Thank you for taking the time to see me, Thomas."

He took her gloved hand and kissed it. "Always my favorite abolitionist and lady."

"Ah, on that you should be careful. Gossip has it you are to marry and I'm sure the future Mrs. McHenry would not care to hear that," she jested only to meet his scowl.

"Well, we are not married yet."

That was a quick response. Intrigued her but she wasn't here for that.

"I do have a problem I fear will require your services."

He offered her a seat before he retook his. "How can I be of service?"

Larissa always liked Thomas. He was courteous,

to the point and all for the cause.

"You met Miss Jaquita Fontaine?"

He gave her a warm smile. "Yes, I met her. In the market one day. Had an issue with Mattie. You know that Irish lass with the stall there?"

"Oh, yes, who doesn't?" Larissa tightened. "Let me guess. She didn't want to sell to her?"

"Exactly. I showed her how that didn't bode well for business." He had a smug look on his face, like he'd just saved a client from a wrongful indictment. Her admiration for him soared.

"Well, she has another situation requiring a correction by a man of your influence."

He leaned forward chin perched at the steeple of his fingertips. "Do tell."

"Her father, Pierre Fontaine of Louisiana, has sent her funds and deposited them in the bank. Well, she went to make a withdrawal, and they simply will not allow her to take any of it."

"For whatever reason?"

"Because she is Black, or mulatto, makes no difference considering." She pulled her fan out and opened it up. "Not without her 'massa' there by her side, despite the fact the account has her name on it, and she had a letter from him saying it was hers."

His lips curled up at the challenge. "Hmmmm interesting. Which bank?"

"First Market Bank and Trust."

He drummed his fingertips on the desktop. "I'm familiar with them. I will need to meet with Miss Fontaine, see her credentials and such for this." He eyed her. "Now, Larissa, does she know you are here on her behalf?"

A nervous twitch caught her eye and a nerve in the cheek on the same side. "Not officially. But I did tell her I'd see what I could do to help her."

He sighed. "Larissa, that girl is a hellion, from what I could tell. Has to be to be here, alone from what I saw, in New York, even Albany, to try to make it on her own."

"Do you know of her father, Pierre Fontaine?"

Thomas shook his head. "I don't have time to read the gossip rags. That is what I have you ladies for."

"He's a very influential and wealthy Southerner. Old Creole family. Apparently, he has recognized her or, at the very least, favored her to grant her such, as she's living in the Fontaine mansion out on Westchester Street. If we could just enlist her in the cause, we might have a fortune come our way."

"You're sounding very devious."

"Thomas, the girl's money is being held from her. Don't you think that's ample cause for aid from a legal expert like yourself?"

Righting himself in the chair, he tossed the pencil stub he'd been whirling around onto the desk. "You are right. Time to go talk to Miss Fontaine."

Larissa smiled.

Jaquita stood in front of the teller, this time feeling more equipped to take him on than last time. As if she had armor on, thanks to Thomas

McHenry III standing just behind her and off to her right. She couldn't help but feel invincible. Here stood a lawyer, argument in hand as it were, to get her access to money that was hers. *Ha!*

She walked up to the window to the same clerk. The young man didn't even look up at first, just sat crouched over his ledger book. Irritated, she cleared her throat after she snapped her fan open and started to wave it.

He looked up, peering at her through his spectacles. "Yes ma'am?"

"I'm here to request a withdrawal."

He raised his brows as he pursed his lips. She figured he remembered her. He slipped her a scrap of paper with a pencil stub. Quickly, she filled in her name and the account it was under, which was also her name.

Staring at the scrap, he glanced up. "And where is Miss Fontaine?"

Her anger started to flare. "I am Miss Jaquita Fontaine."

She got a questioning glance from him. "And you have verification?"

"I beg your pardon?" Again that questioning her legitimacy. Anger started to boil.

"Is your master here? Or a white person of note?"

Fire exploded in her gut. "I am my own person,"

"Yes, I can see that. But we don't normally have Blacks, freedmen or not, simply arrive to take this much out at once."

"Yes, well, I have need of that."

"Ma'am," the clerk started when Thomas

stepped up.

"Excuse me. I'm Thomas McHenry III, Miss Fontaine's attorney. This is her account. Now, fulfill her request."

The clerk glared at Thomas but the lawyer stood his ground. The confidence he exuded was comforting and she found herself taking a side step closer to him. He didn't back down. The boy behind the podium halfway snarled and yanked her request off the working top, fuming as he stormed off. Thomas never moved.

Jaquita studied him in those few moments. When he'd arrived with Mrs. Wainwright to see her, she doubted what they proposed would work. She had insisted she would just write to her father to clear the issue, but Larissa pushed and Thomas backed her up. Now was the time to move, not months from now when bills were past due and her pantry bare. So they'd arrived here, at the bank, determined to win.

Her lawyer was still the most handsome man she'd seen earlier at the market and at the abolitionist hall that night. Even now, in a totally formal occasion, when his professional services were used, he was so dapper, she found her heart skipped a beat. She shut her eyes, working hard to refocus on why she was here to start with. Money. *Her money.*

The clerk returned with a tied envelope and handed it to Thomas. But Thomas refused to take it.

"I'm not Miss Fontaine."

The clerk's cheeks flamed as his eyes narrowed.

With sharp move, he dropped it on the countertop in front of Jaquita without saying a word. His abruptness, the rudeness he displayed infuriated her until she grasped the package and it hit her, she'd won. A sly smile inched across her lips despite her trying to maintain her stoic stance.

"Thank you." She looked at Thomas and caught the glimmer in his eyes, making her smile burst out. She spun to face the door, the swish of her skirts audible in the now quiet lobby and she walked out, back straight, shoulders stiff, fighting to keep herself from dancing.

Outside the door, on the steps to the bank, she couldn't contain it any longer and squealed with delight as she clutched her envelope tightly. A male laugh behind her made her turn and find her lawyer grinning.

"Well done, Miss Fontaine."

"Mr. McHenry, thank you for assisting me." Her cheeks warmed and she hoped she didn't blush as badly as the heat indicated.

He crinkled his nose. "You did all the work. Considering how determined you were, he had no choice. I was just there in case you needed it."

"You're very sweet. I tend to think otherwise, that your presence got the point home. And for that, I'd like to thank you." She knew he was aware that with him at her side, the clerk could not argue against her. The gleam in his dark gaze told her he knew it.

"You are welcome."

"So what do I owe you for this representation?"

He frowned as he offered her his arm, which she took and started walking her down the street. "Owe me? I don't think anything in money."

"No? Since when does a lawyer refuse payment?"

He laughed. It was a deep and seductive laugh, one that pulled her closer. "Okay. How about if I settle for dinner with you?"

That surprised her. "Dinner?" Her voice broke and she mentally stomped her foot at that.

"Well, it's past tea, and late afternoon. Unless you have other plans, I think it would be delightful to dine with you. Maybe consider it a late 'tea' plus." His grin was enticing. Part of her yelled 'no' while 'yes' was more forceful.

"You, Mr. McHenry, are quite the persuader."

He stopped, a winning grin across his face. "Excellent. And here we are. McLaughlin's Club."

She spun a glance at the building they were in front of, realizing she'd paid no notice where they were walking. It was a three-story brick building with stairs leading up to the double-wide black doors with huge brass knockers on the center of each.

"Club? With a name like that, my father would laugh while still stating that was not a place for ladies."

"Understandable. But it is a fine establishment for dining and opened to all." A devilish look came to his face. "Shall we?"

Not sure if she would regret this caving to the

devil, or enjoy more time with this handsome lawyer, Jaquita gave a nod, giving into his infectious grin and praying she came out alive.

*"You are green, it is true, but they are green, also; you are all green alike."*

—Abraham Lincoln response to Union field commander, General Irvin McDowell on the Federal troops early in the war. July 1861

# CHAPTER EIGHT

Thomas hadn't planned to take her to eat. He hadn't planned to do anything other than get her access to her money. An easy job, he decided, and not one to take all his day, which was already crammed with work. But it got him out of the office and eliminated any chance Allison would find him if she so happened to be 'in the area', which was her latest scheme to see him. He decided that might make him a scoundrel to avoid the woman, and perhaps in reality he was, but his anger over his father pressuring him to marry her was slowly killing any desire to see her at all.

Jaquita was another story. When he saw her again, dressed so fine in that lovely yellow gown with its brown ruffles and ribbons, he knew this woman was enticing his attentions more and more.

Inside the Club, he took her to one of the

tables, not far from the French doors that led out to the small garden outside guests could retire too. He wanted to be close to the sun that poured in there, so he could enjoy the sparkle of color off her entrancing bluish-brown eyes. As he held her chair, a wicked sense of winning raced through him. It was a feeling that escaped him as to why, so he did his best to dampen it, though his heartbeat jumbled nonetheless.

As their tea and cakes were served, he asked, "So you're a Fontaine?"

She raised her brows as she bit into the tea cake. He couldn't tell if she was mad or surprised, or maybe even annoyed he asked her.

"Yes. My father is Pierre Fontaine from Bellefountaine Plantation in Louisiana."

That's what he'd guessed. "So he does claim you as his child?"

"Yes." She took a sip of her tea. "Why?"

He sat back. "Many slave owners who father children with a bondswoman rarely acknowledge them, though most everyone knows. You father is different."

"Oui. He favored my mother. But she died when I was very young so he had me raised with his other children. Not entirely unusual. Many times, the white children do play with the slave children, until we all reach the age of knowing our position, as it were." She shrugged. "While the slave children then are separated from the play and move into their future roles on the farm, I was left with my father's other children."

"Fascinating." She had his attention, that was

for sure. "So you know how to read and write as well."

A flash of anger shot across her eyes and faded fast, though the tight jawline remained. "Yes, I know how to read and write and do arithmetic. I was taught how to run a house, just like my white sister was." She put her tea cup down and the china chimed from the forced action. "You're going to tell me you've never met an educated Black woman before?"

He cocked his head to the side, still trying to figure just how mad he'd made her. "I've met a few. Not with the background and resources you have."

"Mais, oui, though that did me no good at the bank." She dabbed at her lips, hiding her moving them as she spewed in French into it.

"I beg your pardon? Was that French?" Her hiding the swear word made him want to laugh.

She blushed. "Oui. I know the tongue. My father and his wife are Creole. They had their white children learn it, and since I was there." She shrugged.

"What did you say?" He wanted to hear her say it.

"It wasn't nice."

"Even better to tell me," he pushed.

"Connard."

He laughed. "I can be."

"You speak French?" She looked shocked.

"Here, in New York state, there's French just north of us in Canada. Many times, we have clients who have situations with them, so…" He let it slide, took a sip of tea and then asked, "Say something more in French."

"Why?" She pulled her fan out and started using it.

"Because I love the way it sounds when you speak it."

She now blushed deep red that made her skin glow. *Damn, she was beautiful!*

"Thomas, what a surprise!"

Instantly, Thomas tightened. Allison. He hadn't noticed her entering. Her excitement only amplified her voice and he recognized it. He stood but so wanted to bite the inside his bottom lip to hold back from making a face that reflected his feelings.

"Miss Lancaster, how nice to see you." He couldn't be rude, though the thought did cross his mind. She sat next to their table, her close friend, Miss Crosslake, next to her. That woman didn't like him, but that was fine with him because he didn't care a wit for her either.

"Oh, Thomas, don't be so formal!" Allison insisted. "I'm just surprised to see you here, and so late in the day." She turned and saw Jaquita and her whole face changed to surprise and shock.

"I didn't know you had company," she stated, her voice edging on jealousy.

"Well, you surprised us. I hadn't had time to introduce you. This is my client, Miss Fontaine. Miss Fontaine, this is Miss Lancaster, and her friend Miss Crosslake."

Jaquita nodded. "Nice to meet you." Her tone was flat.

"I would say the same." She turned to Thomas. "You take clients to late tea?"

"Miss Lancaster, yes I do when we are discussing her situation." He clouded his main reason was to know her. Somehow, he bet that's not what Allison would like. He so wanted to snicker but fought against it.

Allison, though, maintained her cheerfulness, despite the hurt that flashed in her eyes. Her friend, though, gave him a hard look, as if he had betrayed Allison.

"Thomas, it was great to see you. And nice to make your acquaintance, Miss Fontaine." She glanced at her friend. "Miss Crosslake and I must leave. Good bye."

"Miss Lancaster," he tipped his head down as she spun, her skirt and crinoline swirling in her fast pace to leave, with her friend not far behind. Once she was gone, he sat back down. Looking across the table, he found Jaquita with a raised brow. "Allison is a good friend of the family."

His guest looked down her nose at him, her questioning gaze now harder. "Mr. McHenry, that lady is more than a friend of the family."

This was the last thing he wanted to delve into. "Perhaps, though, if you would be so kind, I'd rather we picked up where we were before our interruption." He grinned, hoping his countenance might change her mood. "Now, please, say something more in French."

Jaquita snorted. "Maybe another time. As it is, we should go. Our tea has turned cold."

For once in his life, he wanted to protest loudly

that he didn't want to go because that meant
their time together was over. Inwardly dismayed,
he nodded in agreement, but right as he put his
napkin down, another idea hit him. He stood and
moved her chair for her to get up. As she took his
arm, he walked her to the door.

"I'd like to see you again. Strictly to discuss the
strategy on your banking and," he winked. "To
hear your French. You know, it is divine when
mixed with your Southern accent."

She laughed. "Mais oui, monsieur."

His heart filled with joy. She was stealing his
heart.

*2 days later*

Clarence walked back to the kitchen, parched
and looking for water. Plus, he was pulled
back to talk to Aunt Lila. Too much of what he
saw disturbed him, but then again, he might be
wrong and he believed the cook was the only
other servant who would listen.

Of course, when he arrived in the cooking area,
she wasn't there. He grumbled as he searched for
a cup and found the pitcher.

"And what are you doing in my kitchen?"

Clarence smiled as he took a sip. Aunt Lila. She
always claimed the kitchen hers, though she had
been promoted beyond its realm to manage the
house itself.

"My throat was parched." He drank more.

"You'll get yourself all sick swallowing it like a drowning man!" She pulled the cup from his grasp. "Tsk, tsk!" she poured from another pitcher, one to the left, with the cheesecloth over the opening. "Drink this."

He snorted before he downed the raspberry vinegar tainted water. "Vile stuff," he determined.

"Maybe, but it'll make sure your innards sit right." She yanked an apple from the bowl in front of her and began slicing. "Why don't you tell me why you're really here."

"You know me too well."

She hummed but didn't stop eying him in a questioning state.

"Have you seen our little girl?" He took another sip, trying not to gag on the vinegar taste.

"Miss Jaquita is not 'our little girl', but no, I haven't." She busied herself, now sifting flour with a touch of salt for a crust, he figured, considering the number of apples she had cut.

"She just as well is," he argued back. "She's young enough and naïve enough, too much so for this here town. Wolves wait at every stop for a fawn like her."

Aunt Lila laughed. "Perhaps you're right. But what has you so concerned? Ain't no wolves in this house."

"No, but there's the type that take her time."

"What would you have her do? Wait here till she's 'old enough' you'd let her lose? Stay in this big old house, gardening out there like a house slave?" She kneaded the dough. "When she was caught doin' so, how the town's best here thinkin' poorly of her. No, she's better keeping busy."

"But not with the likes of him." There, he said it. When Aunt Lila looked up with a frown, he knew he'd hit the point dead on. "Oh, you ain't been seein' who she's been tooling with? That lawyer."

Aunt Lila swallowed and went back to her dough. "Mr. McHenry. He's a good man. Part of the abolition group. He got her access to her bank account and been showing her how to deal with issues—"

"Has he now?"

She looked at him, surprised he interrupted her, but he had to. He shook his head.

"He's no good for her."

At that, the cook chuckled. "He's a lawyer. They generally are rather drab fellows, but at least he is dapper in looks to make up for the dullness." She wiped her hands and reached over to squeeze his hand. "It is okay."

"She should be lookin' at helpin' the Society." There, he said it.

"Rather bold remark from a man who never attends a meeting."

"Don't like the people goin'. You know most those white folk don't care. Just fashionable to be part of it." Even hearing his argument in his head, he sounded rightly daft, but he really believed all of what he stated.

"Even Mrs. Wainwright? Or Mrs. Douge? Or half as many more I could name? And what of Jeremiah? He ran all the way north to escape slavery, or do you think all those marks on his back or the one on his face are just made up?"

"No, I reckon not." The small nick near his eye was obvious to see, but the ones on his back were shown one night at the meeting. Clarence wasn't there, but it was the talk of the house since several of the staff had gone.

"So if you don't like the people there, why do you think Miss Jaquita should go?"

"'Cause she's one of us, and from the South and got money. All the running in the world won't change the laws. We both know that." He wiped his mouth. Spitting the words out fast left spittle. "Takes money."

"Yes, money and who you know." Aunt Lila finished patting the crust down into the pie pan. "And her knowing Mr. McHenry is the type of connections needed, so leave them be. It's not like they're eloping."

Clarence choked on his drink. "Good heavens, let's hope not!"

*"All the indications are that this treasonable inflammation—secessionitis—keeps on making stead progress, week by week."*
—George Templeton Strong, Wall Street attorney, Spring 1861

# CHAPTER NINE

Jaquita plucked another strawberry off the dish before her and sucked it into her mouth. Thomas, sitting across from her, laughed. She loved his laughs so she found herself doing silly things like this, of taking a berry off the dessert in front of her with her fingers, and plopping it in between her lips. It was like she had no manners but at the moment, she decided she didn't care. She was enjoying her time with him.

Thomas leaned forward and wiped the cream off her lips. "They may ask us to leave if you continue this behavior."

"I doubt that." She looked down, trying to look contrite but it didn't last.

"How did your shopping go today?" He gave her a wink over the glass of wine.

"I did very good. Amazing how a little bit of confidence plus the money to spend can change people's minds." She spent the early afternoon shopping for a few items. It amazed her he remembered she'd talked about this yesterday. Their discussion on legal items of note had been rather dull, so she figured when he asked her what she'd planned to do for today, it had been for taking her to dinner, nothing more. Most men, she had heard, hardly gave a whim to women's leisure choices, unless it involved them and her shopping hadn't.

"See? I told you that you could get what you want."

"On everything?" She couldn't help but ask. A voice in the back of her head whispered *even if I want you?*

"Unfortunately, probably not." He sighed. "Though I see you could gain great confidence and leadership if directed correctly."

"As in how?"

He spooned a scoop of the berries and cream. "You could help the Anti-Slavery people. That would be worthy cause."

The hair on her neck bristled. "I'm hardly counted by those people. They talk of atrocities."

"Well, I'd bet you saw some while growing up."

She frowned. "Just because I'm from the South and grew up on a plantation with slaves doesn't mean I saw anything along the lines they speak of. No mutilations, no brandings, no isolation boxes, nothing. Just positions and chores."

There was a wrinkle across his forehead, as if that didn't sit right with him. She tossed that idea aside. Well, she was there. Her family, though white and a bit broken, were not abusers! Determined to correct his assumption, she looked back at him and found he gave her a half-grin with his glass of wine raised.

"To the Fontaines!"

Unsure of his meaning, she decided to just raise her stemware to meet his and as they clanged, she saw mischief in his eyes. Downing her sip, she asked, "Whatever is going on in that mischievous mind of yours?"

"Dance with me."

"Dance? There's no one dancing," she glanced around and then frowned. "There's no one here." She turned back to him right as he stood, offering for her hand. "What did you do?"

At that moment, as if on cue, a handful of men carrying string instruments walked in and set up on the side. She took his hand slowly, wondering what was happening.

"They needed a place to practice," he told her with a shrug. "The owner here took pity, considering, and let them in here."

"So they practice in dress clothes," she noted as he spun her in front of him.

"Yes, it is truly odd, I have to agree."

Taking his hand as they stood in position to dance, she gave him a sharp eye. His attempt to look innocent made her laugh. "You planned this."

"Perhaps." The strings started and he stepped to the right. "I wanted to dance. And I was sure you would, too."

The music was lovely and she fully let herself go, following his lead, which was so easy. They danced the jig, and galloped for the trot and finally settled into a waltz. She had to admit, dancing with him was so easy and enjoyable, she let herself relax, realizing this was the first time since moving north that she had.

"You appear to like this," he whispered.

"You, sir, are quite correct," she replied. "Thank you."

He gazed into her eyes. He was a full head taller than her and, in his arms, she felt safe, an emotion she never truly felt. His blue eyes were dark, almost navy in color, and so intense. It was like a flame, one that spread through to her and her soul drank it in.

In the now candlelit room, with the music floating, the scent of lilies in the air, all seemed perfect. His steps slowed and he pulled her closer. Jaquita's mouth turned dry and she licked her lips right as her stomach flipped.

He pulled his hand away from her lower back when they came to a stop. He tipped her chin up as he lowered his head and took her lips in a kiss. It was a light touch, almost like feathers across her yet she could taste the bourbon on his lips mixed with the cream from her strawberry. It was an alluring taste and she wanted more. She rose on her toes, trying to reach his height as he slowly pulled back. Separated by mere inches, he gazed at her with his dark eyes and a lazy grin.

Irritated and hungry for more, she again stood and reached up to join him again in a kiss. This time, he didn't pull back but met her half way. His mouth covered hers and he tried with his tongue to gain entrance inside, his masculine body becoming harder as he strained to kiss her deeply.

Inside her head, a distance voice yelled for her to stop, that he was white and no good would ever come from this! Wasn't her life ample proof mixing didn't work? But she silenced that voice as her lips parted.

With a growl, he devoured her, pulling her tighter into his embrace. As their tongues danced, she knew deep down inside everything had changed.

*Next Day*

Thomas sat, listening to his friend Frederick Wilson continue his oratory about the future. His musings intrigued Thomas, so it took him a few minutes to realize what he was saying.

"So you've been touting *my* worthiness to become a senator? I thought this was about you running."

Frederick rolled back on his heels and laughed loudly. "Me? Hardly. Merchants and scribes do not do well in politics. However, attorneys do very well."

Thomas stood and began to pace. "I have made comments about running, though for this election, it may be too soon to throw my hat into the ring."

"Good grief, it ain't! Look, that scalawag

McDougal just came from Ireland, barely here long enough to be understandable, let alone able to vote! And, you know as well as I do that the Irish want the darkies gone, lock, stock and barrel, back to Africa! Anything but up here, claiming they'll be out of work for the freedmen who'd take scratchings to live, not that those papists aren't at that level anyway."

He did have a point. In this district, the only man he'd oppose was an Irishman, James McDougal, though he'd been here in the states for years and an American citizen roughly a decade ago. But Frederick was right. The Irish didn't want the possibility of more freedmen up in New York for fear they would be hired over the Irish. Rumors flew that the Irish were nothing more than papists and drunks and with a few who fit the bill for the latter, it was becoming harder and harder for them to find shelter and work. A job a senator could help with, along with freeing the slaves.

"So, tell me then, how am I faring?"

Frederick grinned. "Pretty good, I think. Your status of helping all is duly noted, your participation in the Anti-Slavery Society is popular and your engagement to Miss Lancaster is the frosting on your celebratory cake!"

He stared out the window of his office, looking down at the markets below. Allison. His father still pushed the union. He did give it some thought, except Jaquita always interrupted those ideas. Last night flooded him mind. She was beautiful, the dusky hue of her skin made her like a goddess in his eyes. She danced so gracefully he became more enthralled with her. And that kiss…

"So I figure you're a shoo-in for the seat!"

Thomas turned his attention back to now with a frown as he slunk back into his desk chair.

"You will run, right? I'm not out there, just wasting mine and my team's voices for a ghost?"

The group of ten lads, really young gentlemen that Frederick had rounded up, had also begun to spread his name and worth. He drummed his fingertips across his desktop.

"All right, all right. You won. I will put myself on the ballot."

"Huzzah!"

He prayed that was the right choice.

*"If destruction be our lot, we must ourselves be its author and finisher. As a nation of freemen, we must live through all time, or die by suicide."*
—Abraham Lincoln, 1838

# CHAPTER TEN

Another day of shopping, but with his money this time. It made Jaquita giggled. As the carriage rambled down the street, more bumpy than smooth, she did her best to hide her laughter and averted her gaze away from her companion. Unfortunately, that made it even worse, because she knew he was watching her.

"What is so funny?" Thomas finally asked.

"You. Us. Everything." She couldn't stop the laugh, even when not looking at him. Out of the corner of her eye, she saw him fight not to grin.

"I think we are quite lovely."

"Lovely? Do men think that way?" An intriguing thought, she tilted her head.

"We think in all sorts of ways."

His words rolled out in a deep, dark tone that made her blood race. The memory of that kiss made her mouth water. Before she had time to think right, the words rolled out of her mouth, "You will stay for dinner?"

He gave her a mischievous half-grin. The air between them thickened because she couldn't move, nor take her gaze off him. She bit her bottom lip after what seemed like eternity, waiting, hoping when he finally answered, "I'd love to."

A breeze washed over her, one filled with relief and excitement and she grinned. "Excellent."

At the house, the driver opened the door and Thomas left first then spun to lift her out of the conveyance. His hands rested on her waist to guide her to the ground but the fire they left at the top of her hips nearly undid her. She muttered a thank you and quickly strode toward the front door, telling Clarence that Mr. McHenry was joining her for dinner. With those orders given, she left him with her cloak and bonnet and led Thomas back to the library.

He walked into the room behind her but left the door open, for which she was thankful. Her heart was thudding wildly and the fact that she'd just issued orders like she was the grand mistress of the house scared and elated her all at once. Or was her forwardness due to him?

"So do you have many guests?" he causally asked as he walked to the sideboard. Picking up the wine bottle, he tilted his head in questioning form.

"Yes, that would be lovely." Wine might slow her heart down, she hoped, but then it hit her how it sounded like she answered the first part. "And no, I don't have guests to speak of."

He handed her a glass of the red wine. "I didn't

think so. You rattled off those commands like you are a practicing court lawyer or a politician."

"Oh, my, no! I apologize for being so rude!" Her cheeks heated instantly from embarrassment.

He gestured for them to sit as she collected her thoughts—and her wits—and took a seat on the settee. He took the side chair. She swallowed the lump in her throat.

"You are not rude, my dear. Perhaps a bit uncomfortable at the moment, but we will muddle through that and you will relax." He raised his wineglass. "To a beautiful hostess, who will honor all of us in New York."

Again, her cheeks burned. "Truly, a nice gesture—"

"For toasts, you simply raise your glass and then take a sip." He looked on the verge of laughing.

She closed her mouth and snorted. Blinking, she refocused on him, raised her glass in return to his and then sipped as he did. "Thank you."

As they put their glasses down, she noticed he sat at ease, even his face was light except for his eyes. They gave her an intent stare. *What was going on in his mind?*

"Did you enjoy our day?"

That wasn't what she was expecting from those stern eyes and the reflection they gave, but the man did sound curious.

"I did. Immensely. Thank you for that as well."

"I just wanted to make sure you didn't have any other issues from the shop clerks." His half-smile returned as he looked away for a moment. "They gave me a time, as it were."

"I wasn't aware you had taken a turn to run for office."

He shrugged. "It seemed logical. Better to take the fight to Congress."

Jaquita frowned. "What fight?"

"For emancipation, of course." He took another drink of the wine.

"Oh." She wasn't sure what to say. How did one congratulation or wish one well for a job she didn't understand? It sounded unpleasant, or that was how she saw politicians, thanks to her father's views.

"Don't you want your people free?"

"My people? You mean, the slaves? Of course." She squirmed a bit.

"Then you'll surely join the Anti-Slavery group. We could surely use your support."

She gulped.

Clarence left the coat and wraps to another servant so he could head back to the kitchens, his mind filling with disturbing thoughts. With every step, the elder butler became more and more troubled by what he'd witnessed. But they could be too late.

His mind still clouded with troubling thoughts, he turned the corner in the back hallway and walked straight into Aunt Lila's kitchen. "Aunt Lila, we have a situation on our hands!"

The cook looked up from the table she stood at, cutting bread. The waft of dinner wrapped around the room and made his mouth water with hunger but it was dinner that drove him here. She gave him a questioning glance before returning her attention to the cutting board.

"Why? What has happened now?"

"We have guests for dinner."

Aunt Lila chuckled. "And that is a problem?"

"You'll find it so when I tell you who." He paused and grew irritated when she rolled her eyes and returned to her food preparation. "It's that lawyer."

"Clarence, please. There are more lawyers than necessary in this town. Who?"

"That white boy. Mr. McHenry." He huffed loudly, a little miffed she didn't even trifle at the announcement.

"I see," she answered, finishing putting the bread on a tray with the whipped butter. "Nothing wrong with that. He's been helping Miss Jaquita settle in here."

"Oh, he's helping her settle in just fine," Clarence smirked. "I saw their eyes and how her cheeks be all red. Ain't right to let her be alone with him."

Aunt Lila collected her vegetables from the pot, the steam raising off them, making her face glisten. "Did Mika set another set place at the table?"

"Of course, he did! That ain't the problem."

She sighed. "Clarence, let it be. I'm sure she was just being polite. He took her to the stores today, making sure they treated her right. He's taking on taming New York for her, so—"

"He's doin' more than that!" the butler blustered.

"You know he runnin' for office."

"So I hear."

"Well, he trying to get influence, toting a freewoman around, as if he cares about freeing us Blacks."

Aunt Lila snorted. "He does. He's part of the Albany's *and* New York City's Anti-Slavery Societies. I heard from Mrs. Wainwright, he offers his counsel at a reduced rate."

"And what is he offering our Jaquita?"

Aunt Lila stopped. Clarence was elderly and set in his ways, that everyone knows their place and should stay there. But rarely did she ever see him this upset.

"Clarence," she started, her voice low and sympathetic. "Miss Jaquita has had a rough time—"

"Ha!" Clarence snorted, his face still contorted in muddled anger. "Rough, but with money. So hard!"

"Yes, money she could not get to, and Mr. McHenry has been nothing but courteous and respectful in getting her access to it." She rubbed her hands against her apron as she pulled herself upright. "He is also supposed to get her to join the Society and perhaps, be a contributor and maybe speak."

"Contributor of what? That money is her pappy's. And speaker for what? Living on a big ole Southern plantation? 'Cause you know, no one has ever whipped that girl, nor caused her harm. You've seen how they've treated her. Like kin!"

"Yes, well, they have treated her well, for a mulatto child. Mr. Fontaine has a liking for her, that's for sure, enough to send her here and on her own and it's that wealth they're hoping she'll share."

"Just don't like this."

Aunt Lila patted his arm. "It will be all right. 'Sides, I hear Mr. McHenry about to get engaged himself. Then he won't be courtin' Miss Jaquita like you think."

Jaquita laughed. "You can't be serious! He wanted you to what?"

Thomas chuckled. "Well, as long as Jonathan was alive and being raised to follow my father, what was I, the second son, to do?"

"Head west? To where?" She frowned. "Chicago?"

"Nah, that's not 'west'. Guessing the likes of Kansas."

Jaquita bit her tongue, realizing she had no idea really where Kansas was. Geography wasn't something the tutors taught the Fontaine children, meaning she didn't pick it up from them or trying to listen to the classes from afar. But she recalled a globe in the library that she'd go inspect later.

"So what happened?"

Thomas took a drink of his wine and gave her one of is half-smiles, the type she suddenly found very attractive. "Well, Jonathan couldn't pass the class in law. My way of thinking is my brother didn't want all the tedium a law office can bring but, the lure of the west, it grabbed his attention. All newspapers wrote tales of open land and little law, so he sprang for it." He dabbled his lips with the napkin. "Took the maid with him too. An Irish lass named Kate."

Jaquita couldn't help but laugh.

"So my father was less than pleased. Formally disowned him, treated him as if dead, and took me under his wing to train to follow him."

"Is that what you wanted? To follow him as a lawyer?"

Thomas shrugged. "I'd been helping Jonathan with his studies, so I basically had the training. Took me nothing to get through the classes and here I am."

"Hmmmmm," she hummed, taking a bite of her cake. It melted in her mouth, just like her insides inflamed in his presence. The room was way too hot.

"I wanted to ask you a question."

She looked up, barely able to swallow the second bite she had inhaled as a way to divert her attention off him.

"Will you attend the Anti-Slavery Ball Saturday?"

Jaquita rolled her lips inward. She'd seen the invitation. "I hadn't decided." That was a safe answer, mainly because it was the truth.

"I'd be so honored if you did. It is a big fund raiser for the Society and heaven knows, we need it for the fight to set your people free."

He looked so begging, pleading her to go. But her insides were torn. How was she to explain it? She'd never really seen nor felt enslaved, though even to think that was wrong. So since she couldn't feel the pull, she'd ignored the Society that made her uncomfortable. And yet, the look in his eyes, so hoping she would go, and hopefully, he'd be there. That made her excited and nervous all at once.

"I hadn't decided."

"I've had a dress ordered for you."

Surprised, she frowned. "Since when?"

He snorted, fighting back a smile and losing. "Well, we were out shopping today, and did go through a couple of seamstress's establishments."

Shocked, she dropped her fork. She couldn't breathe. It was like the air was turned thin and she was enclosed in a box. Quickly, she reached for the fan that she'd set next to her plate and fanned herself rapidly. Trying to calm herself, she barely heard his chair screech as he pushed it back and raced to her side.

"Are you all right?" he asked, touching her forehead.

"Yes," she finally muttered as embarrassment took control and her breathing returned. "I'm just surprised. You've done enough for me as it is."

"Think of it as a gift. A gift to help a beautiful lady and one I'd love to have on my arm, to twirl about the dance floor." He kissed the back of her hand. The touch of his lips sparked a fire deep inside her.

"Yes," the answer came without her realizing it. Blinking hard, she continued. "I will go and thank you for the gift."

"Fabulous!" He lifted her out of the chair and spun her in the space behind the table.

It was a quick turn and his jovial spirit made her laugh. Once around and then they stopped. She looked at him, realizing she didn't understand him at all. The twinkle in his eyes amused her, enticed her and scared her, all at once. Then he did the unthinkable. He swooped her up into his arms and kissed her hard.

Her heart pounded and she molded against his body. Wrapped in his embrace, she mewled softly, giving in to his request to devour her mouth. The moment she opened her lips, he growled. As he kissed her, she took all of him in and found her body begging for more.

Then, he pulled away from her lips and gently let her down. They both panted, breathless, their eyes glued on each other.

"Miss Jaquita," he started formally, inhaling deeply. "I was told your dress should be ready tomorrow. She will come here for the final fitting."

He stepped back, tugging at her hand till the last second when heels were heard coming down the hallway toward them.

"I'm glad you stayed for dinner," she stated loud enough for the oncoming servant and the hint it was better he left.

He winked at her. "Thank you. Till I see you

again." And he was gone.

She sunk into the chair, finding herself confused. *Who is this man?*

*"Our new government is founded on the opposite idea of the equality of the races...Its corner stone rests up the great truth that the Negro is not equal to the white man."*
—Confederate Vice President Alexander H. Stephens, 1861

# CHAPTER ELEVEN

Larissa walked around the grand room again, checking for another time that the flowers and garland were set right, candelabras sufficiently lit and the string band's staging area was arranged. This was the largest fund raiser the Society had set for the year and it had to be perfect, in order to keep funds coming, or that was the way she viewed it. The price to attend was four times larger than last year, and with the band playing for free, she hoped they made a lot to fund the cause.

"Larissa, dear, it is set perfectly," her husband confided her.

"Darling, with the upcoming election and what has happened out west with Kansas, we desperately need the money. I need this to be a night to remember to keep it coming in."

He laughed. "You worry too much. The

movement has picked up steam, especially since the passage of that abhorrent bill."

The Runaway Slave Act had been enacted in the North as an answer to get popular sovereignty in Congress, the idea of the incoming territories to determine if they were free or slave states. The North had been all for it, convinced the new territories like Kansas and Nebraska, would come in free. The South grumbled, demanding the number of senators remain equal between the north and south and that this act would outweigh the balance. Allowing Southern slave catchers to come north to the free states to capture runaways softened the blow, at the expense of the anti-slavery citizens, some of who housed the runaway slaves. Now, they'd be charged with hiding a fugitive and successfully closing some of the safe places for them. It only made Larissa scream, which did nothing helpful. The Society, though, could.

"Yes, we could," she muttered, rearranging another leaf in the display. "If we all agreed and got along."

"We all agree slavery is wrong," he countered.

She sighed, shaking her head but looked at him with a weary half-smile. "Perhaps, but there are too many with other ideas."

The musicians arrived, taking their spots right as she and Mr. Wainwright positioned themselves near the entrance. He picked up her hand and kissed the back of it.

"I'll be more interested in the celebrating with you after the party," he whispered.

She flushed right as their doorman announced the first guests. It'd be a long night before he got his wish, she thought.

Jaquita fiddled with her skirt folds again, trying to calm her nerves, which had suddenly frayed. When the carriage pulled up to the Wainwrights mansion, and all the carriages pooled around the front with the lights streaming from the windows, she realized this ball wasn't casual in a way. Not that she thought it would be, however, the numbers surprised her and made her anxious.

When the carriage driver opened the door, it took her a minute to swallow the lump in her throat, gather her wrap and reticule and fan, taking a handful of her long skirt to clear the way to step out. As the door closed behind her and the front door opening to the ball glared in front of her, thoughts of flight came to her head. *No, she'd not flee!* Thomas had given her a new dress for this, begged her to go, so she would and thank him for it personally.

At the door, the butler didn't frown but simply asked her name and directed her forward.

"Miss Fontaine," he announced loudly as she walked into the ballroom. She cringed as many glanced her way.

"Oh, Jaquita!" Mrs. Wainwright took her hands and squeezed them. "Don't look so worried. James always announces the guests for events like this." Her warm smile gave Jaquita a moment to catch her breath and return the look.

"I take it you haven't been to many formal balls?" Mr. Wainwright asked.

"No, not really. There were a few, usually part of house parties that lasted for days. Everyone knew each other, so formal announcements were not given that I heard. I, of course, didn't get to go."

She caught Mrs. Wainwright jab him in the ribs. "Duane, please. You realize the South is a bit more spread. I should've remembered that myself. Forgive me and welcome to tonight's festivities."

"Thank you and please," she begged. "I will recover."

The hostess frowned. "You came alone? I thought—"

"Miss Jaquita!"

They turned at the call. It was Jeremiah and he was quickly walking towards them.

"Please forgive me. I was planning on escorting you here, but my plans got disarrayed." His brows furrowed as he gave her the complex expression. "If you will, I'd be honored to have the first dance." He held out his hand for her.

Jaquita frowned, not recalling even a word from him of escort. She thought it would be Thomas. She opened her mouth but never got a word out.

"What a delightful recovery! Yes, please, you two go and dance. Duane and I will join you shortly." Mrs. Wainwright waved them off as another attendee arrived.

"Come, I will take you from this madness," Jeremiah whispered, leading her to the dance floor. They added onto a grouping, making the four couples complete for the dance right as the music started. "This is an easy dance," he whispered. "Just follow along."

It took Jaquita a few steps to catch onto the movements as they roved up the line and back down. When she met him on the third part of the dance, in the few seconds they had, she frowned.

"You appear a bit frazzled, sir."

He snorted. "Runs at night can do that."

His answer made no sense. Runs? It puzzled her but before she could ask, they broke apart to dance intricately down the line before meeting again.

"You ran? Who runs at night?"

"The Railroad," he answered and again, they separated. Still confused, she barely made the steps right because her mind wanted him to explain further.

"Will you explain yourself?" she murmured on the next meeting.

He only grinned.

Soon the dance ended and as they bowed and curtseyed, she begged him to elaborate.

"What railroad? You work for the railway?" She wanted to stomp her foot but refrained as he took her to the punch table.

Handing her a cup, he replied, "No, not the railroads. I help the Underground line."

She frowned. "The runaway slave train?"

Now he laughed. "Yes, the runaway slave train. Nicely put." He raised his glass like a toast.

"That's dangerous! Why would you do that?" She'd heard faintly of the Underground Railroad. Down South, the mere suggestion was buried but the slaves whispered of it. "And with the Fugitive Slave Law, you could get killed doing so!"

"*Shhhhh*," he took her hand. "I can be pretty sly when I need to be. And it is a rewarding experience."

She frowned. "I don't see how."

Jeremiah frowned as he took a sip of the punch. "Gaining freedom after a life as a slave is celebratory. And everyone deserves to be free."

Jaquita raised her brows as she downed her punch. The cherry-flavored drink was too sweet, she decided. Putting her glass down, she realized Jeremiah was glaring at her.

"You act as if freedom is nothing."

"Oh, heavens, no." She brushed aside his remark. "I'm sure whoever you helped is grateful. I just never seen nor heard of such commotion at home."

Jeremiah stood speechless. He'd spent most of his time helping others of his kind achieve escape from the bonds of slavery, knowing that he risked his life and freedom itself in doing so and it was worth that risk. But this woman, a Southern mulatto, raised by her white father, appeared indifferent to the system. How? Why?

It took him a minute to curb in his anger. Blowing up at her here would get him nowhere. He had to keep his focus on her wealth and how that'd help the cause. And find a way to curb the dawning attraction.

"I have a hard time believing you've missed this.

Nor do I believe you lived in bliss down there in Louisiana. You do realize the worst slave market is in New Orleans, right? That all the slaves sold there have a soul death."

She startled, her brows furrowing. "Soul death?"

"Yes, when they get thrown on the marches south, from whatever circumstances, it means they'll never return, never see the people they've grown to love. Their 'home' with fellow bondsmen."

She looked away. "That seems a bit over much."

He stood there, shock ravaging through his veins. Susan Douge believed the girl had buried the lies she was told and hid from her memories of slavery. All he could determine was she was right and it made him sick. How could he make Jaquita understand her 'family' was no better than any of the others? Apparently, she'd been sheltered from the worst, because who could hide that?

Steeling his shoulders, he figured it was time he helped her move the rocks blocking her memories. Taking her glass, right as the string band started the chords for another dance, he said, "Jaquita, I—"

"Miss Fontaine, I've been looking everywhere for you."

Jeremiah and Jaquita looked up. Anger surged through Jeremiah as Thomas McHenry was at her side, taking her hand to kiss.

"Dance with me," he offered. Then he saw Jeremiah. "You don't mind if I steal her away?"

Still furious, Jeremiah realized now was not the time to destroy her evening and maybe never help the Society. Saved from her past, Jeremiah wished he could save her from this vermin. He shook his head.

"No, we had just had a bit of punch. Miss Jaquita, I'll be here later, if you so desire."

"Thank you Jeremiah." She smiled, right at McHenry as he led her away.

Jeremiah's vision narrowed. He should warn her of the up-and-coming senator, that he wasn't what he appeared to be, despite his aid to the cause. A cause she appeared indifferent to…His blood starting to boil, on top of being worn out from helping that runaway, he went to get a real drink and plan how he would tell her the truth.

Jaquita couldn't understand why Jeremiah was getting so worked up, though he'd done his best to hide it. He helped runaway slaves, that she accepted, but what exactly was driving his temper, one he also worked to hide miserably.

"You look beautiful."

Thomas's words caught her attention and she smiled. "Thank you. Your gift is very lovely."

"Ah, it beckoned your name. That silk screamed it when we walked past the shop. How could I deny it?" His eyes sparkled off his smile and it made her insides tighten.

The music played was a waltz and when Thomas spun her around the room in his arms, her blood rushed. There was something about this man that caught her attention and the longer she was with him, the stronger it became.

Then, he stumbled. It was slight, but enough to catch them both off-guard.

"Apologies," he whispered. "I lost count in the steps, your beauty demanding my full attention."

That made her laugh. "You, sir, are an oaf, in the disguise of a man who wants to dance."

"An oaf? Hmmmm." He bent a little closer. "Be careful. Oafs eat pretty ladies for dessert."

A bubble of laughter spilled out of her lips. "Duly noted, sir."

As the music faded at the end of the dance, he slowly turned them in the final steps, drawing her closer. Her hands rested on muscled shoulders, and now, her breathing became harder as she realized his chest was rock hard, demonstrating how he was strong enough to protect her. She blinked. Why would she think that, she wondered.

He pulled her hand to his lips at the end of the dance and asked in an enchanting tone, "Where do I take you now? Did you come with that stout freedman or were you escorted by another?"

"Why does that matter?" Her heart was racing so fast, she was sure he knew.

"Oh, my dear Miss Jaquita, the rules are very clear. I must return you from where I collected you and that must surely be with another, as a woman as pretty as you should not be left alone to the wolves that lurk near by." His brows rose as the skin around his eyes wrinkled.

"I'm afraid I created my own dilemma," she answered, finding herself playing with the handkerchief she'd pulled from her pocket hidden deep in the skirt. "I came unchaperoned."

"Oh, dear, no! That can not be abided. I shall offer my services in the wake of your missing ones."

"I couldn't ask you—"

"I insist." Taking her to the side of the room, he hailed a servant and obtained two of the wineglasses.

She realized she had pulled her fan out and started cooling herself. With him present, though, she doubted that'd ever happen.

"Here, my lady."

She smiled and took the wineglass, bringing it to her lips slowly. Perhaps the alcohol would help calm her nerves, which at the moment, were dancing dangerously out of control.

"What of your party?" she asked in return.

"My party." He took a sip out of glass. "I, too, came alone, though for a man, that isn't an issue."

It was then a trio came off the dance floor after a rousing gallop, and they were laughing over something, enough so they didn't seem to notice Jaquita or Thomas and the gentleman of the group tried at the last moment to swerve past them but it was too late. Thomas couldn't move fast enough to get out of their way. As the lady on the side of them bumped into Thomas, Thomas stumbled and his wine leaped from his glass and landed squarely on Jaquita's skirts.

"Oh, I am so sorry!" the lady put her gloved hand over her mouth, horrified.

Thomas recovered from his near stumble and managed to catch the stemware before it fell to the floor, but its contents were gone. The red wine punch now left a lingering stain down the cream folds of Jaquita's new gown.

"Jaquita, I'm so sorry," he murmured, pulling his handkerchief out of his pocket to try to stop the drip down the silk but it was too late.

The threesome steered away at Thomas's suggestion, but Jaquita stood staring at the skirt, horrified and fascinated at the pattern the wine left on the fabric.

"We need to get you out of here," he added.

"It is a disaster," she managed to spit out. "I think the dress is ruined." Her vision blurred. She fisted her free hand as despair wanted to take hold. His beautiful gift to her, this stunning cream and yellow silk ball gown now had a red-streak on her front left side. Red. She was on the verge of tears when he took her hand on his arm and turned them toward the door.

"*Shhh* darling," he whispered, taking her hand and leading her toward the ballroom exit in the back.

Fighting not to cry and have tear stains on the bodice as well, she dabbed the corner of her eyes with the lacy handkerchief in her free hand. It took a minute to get it under control and she could see where he was taking her.

The room was dark except for the glow coming from the fireplace embers. He told her to stay still as he went and got a switch to light the end there and then turned to use it to light a lamp. As the warm light spread across the room, Jaquita saw the room was filled with a sitting area, a harp and books. She frowned.

"Where are we?"

"In the back parlor, or as Larissa calls it, her music room." He chuckled, walking back to her. "Here, take a seat."

She sat on the settee, still confused. "My dress."

"Yes, I know." He arranged the skirt fabric to find the stain. "Wait here." And he vanished.

Jaquita sighed, finding herself growing irritated. The lovely dress was ruined so she should leave. No point being here with a soiled garment. She didn't need his assistance leaving, so she folded her fan and poised to get up when he reappeared through the side door, carrying a pitcher and linen.

"Where do you think you're heading?"

"I see no reason to stay with this disgrace. I can quietly leave—"

"And miss my magic?" he tempted, putting his goods down and returning her to the settee. "I'll have you know I have one of the best butlers in the county, maybe even in the country. Stain removal extraordinaire!"

As he adjusted her skirt again to expose the stain, he dipped the rag in the pitcher.

"Truly?"

"Wait. You'll see." He wiped at the dress with the wet rag. Lo and behold, she saw the red lighten and, after a few more swipes, disappear, leaving a wet streak in its place.

"How did you do that?"

He leaned back, a devilish grin on his face. "For that feat, I demand a price."

"Excuse me?"

"You heard me." He chortled. "I saved your new gown. For that, I want a kiss."

*"War is the remedy our enemies have chosen, and I say let us give them all they want; not a word of argument, not a sign of let-up, no cave in till we are whipped—or they are."*
—General William T. Sherman, 1864

# CHAPTER TWELVE

Thomas had a wild array of emotions swirling inside him and everything was contradicted. He so wanted to whisk the lovely lady away from a possible social flaw yet the animal inside him wanted to devour her. The quiet between them as she took in his request grew. He knew it was insane to bring her back here but his intentions were pure. Stains like that could be conquered if acted quickly on, except now, he couldn't help but wonder if the ulterior motives hadn't been the driving cause all along. That realization made him sit upright and forcibly push the thought to the back of his mind.

She rolled her bottom lip in even as a smile threatened to stop her. So, she was amused at his request? That intrigued him more, for most white girls, he'd hear a swoon or some other malarkey like that, but not from this gem sitting across from him.

"A kiss?" With one eyebrow raised in question, a smile hinted and he saw her now hazel eyes turn dark. "Well, come and meet me part way."

His insides tightened even as he stood to fall to her command. He blood was racing, his ears pounding. In two short steps, he was next to her, scooping her off the settee to reach him better. He bent to reach her lips, the contact setting off fires inside him he knew he couldn't squelch. Her sweet petal mouth yielded to his attempt to invade her deep. She tasted of the champagne punch and strawberries, a delight he yearned for more of. As he wrapped his arms around her, pulling her up next to him, he swore he could feel each stay of her corset against his chest and the sway of her skirts as their closeness pushed her crinoline back. She was warm and sweet and the animal inside him roared.

She met his invasion of her mouth with a voracity that surprised him. Her tongue danced with his and even traced the inside of his mouth. She was a seductress, a siren, luring him closer and closer. His hardened member pushed against the constraint of his trousers, and rested close to, he hoped, the apex of her thighs. All he wanted was a taste and now, he was overwhelmed with desire. He had to break the kiss, needed to, but found he was too weak to do so.

Jaquita, though, did the honors and pulled back. She was panting, her lips swollen from his and her deep breaths made her breasts rise against the bodice neckline and that made him harder. Then she licked her bottom lip. He was done. *Damn!*

With his member throbbing painfully, he stepped back.

"Please accept my apologies. I fear I let myself get out of control."

"No, it wasn't your fault." She flattened her palms against her skirt and he saw the tension in her arms and how tight her jawline was. But when her hand hit the damp fabric, she stopped. "I appreciate your aid in removing the spot. I just feared I let our kiss get out of hand."

*She feared his animalistic behavior was all her fault?* He wanted to laugh but held it in. "It is anything but your doing. I was out of line asking for a kiss."

Now, she broke into a smile. "Well, then, perhaps we should return before anyone notices we're missing."

He agreed but did nothing. Neither did she. The air turned thick again. And then, in a moment's notice, he took her back into his arms and bent her backwards with a growl.

Allison returned to Thomas's table, where his parents sat during the dance, and thanked her dance partner, trying desperately to *shoo* him off. Freed, she inhaled deeply and gave the McHenrys a smile. Then she noticed Thomas was vacant. Inwardly, she groaned.

"You look exhausted, my dear," Mrs. McHenry said, making Allison bite the inside of her lip, trying to pull herself upright and animated.

"Mr. Farland is not the best on the dance floor," Mr. McHenry chortled. "You will recover, rest assured."

She laughed. "Oh, thank you, sir. I was afraid it was me." She picked up the champagne glass from the servant who stopped by with a tray full.

"Mr. and Mrs. McHenry."

They turned and found Jeremiah walking up.

"Why, Mr. Johnson, what a pleasant surprise!" Thomas's mother chimed as Jeremiah took her offered hand and kissed it. "Miss Lancaster, may I introduce you to Jeremiah Johnson, one of the major movers of the Albany Anti-Slavery Society. Jeremiah, this is Miss Lancaster and the future Mrs. McHenry III."

"Pleasure to meet you," Jeremiah said to Allison with a big grin, one which she returned with her same remark. But Thomas's mother jumped right back in.

"Enjoying the turn out?"

"Yes. Pleasantly surprised we could pull such a large gathering. Now if the funds equal the numbers, we will make huge progress this year." He grinned ear to ear.

"Speaking of donations, let me steal my wife and we'll go to make ours." Thomas McHenry rose, gathering his wife off her chair. "Will you keep Miss Lancaster company until we return?"

"It would be my pleasure."

Allison bit her tongue and forced her smile to return, now trapped with the eager abolitionist.

"Miss Lancaster, I understand this is your first time to visit one of our events."

She turned and faced him. He wasn't much taller than her and she guessed he wasn't too bad to look at, though she rarely paid attention to the freedmen. Yet, she did note his use of language was proper and that pleased her.

"Yes. I came as a surprise for Thomas, though I've only caught a glimpse at him. On the dance floor, before Mr. Farland stepped on my toe." She still grimaced as it still throbbed from the stomping, though she refused to sit at the moment. "My driver got lost on the way here. Partially my mistake. I said the wrong street." She shrugged. She'd actually gone to the McHenry's townhouse in the hope of catching him there, but was too late.

"Well, he has been out socializing," Jeremiah chuckled. "I've heard rumor that he is running for the senate?"

She tilted her chin up with pride. "Yes, indeed he is."

"Splendid idea. He's done so much for the cause."

She could barely swallow the knot in her throat. She glanced about the room, still not seeing her future husband. What she did see made her shift her weight with a nervous energy.

"I had no idea this was as big an evening as it is for your type."

Jeremiah nearly choked on the champagne he'd just sipped. Her words at the end of her statement stung like a whip across his back, a memory he'd spent the last year trying to bury. Pushing the emotion down, he forced a smile.

"True, for most men, dancing is always a scary proposition. What if we ruin a dress, are clumsy, twirl you too hard or too fast?" He shrugged, working to appear casual while assessing her view.

She laughed. It was a wonderful sound and cleared out his tension. Plus, it animated her face, making her beautiful.

"Oh, yes, that would be an issue I had never thought of." She took a sip out of her glass and after swallowing the champagne, she frowned. "This is my first visit here. I truly believe that slavery is an abomination and truly a sinful act. They need to be set free."

He loved to see how the peculiar institution set her on fire. It'd take fire to destroy the South's views on their chattel, though not the type John Brown had attempted. The staunch abolitionist, who took over Harper's Ferry Arsenal with his sons and freed blacks, believed the local slaves would quickly join their cause to burn slavery out of the South, but he failed and paid for that attempt with his life.

"That is what we are all fighting for." He tilted his head. "Your friend, Mr. McHenry, is a strong supporter of our cause."

"Yes, I'm well aware of that. And he's not my 'friend', but fiancé."

"Truly? Well, congratulations!"

She blushed, her gaze darting around her. "We haven't formally announced it yet, so if you'd be so kind to keep mum on it."

"Certainly, my lips are sealed."

She smiled broader.

"With him as senator, a lot could be done toward that end."

"Yes, yes it could." The enthusiasm in her tone faltered. "We need to free them all and return them to Africa."

His heart skipped a beat. "Africa?"

"Well, of course. That's where you all came from. The slavers stole you from your home, so surely, you'd rather return. I mean, why come north? This isn't home." She shuddered. It was barely noticeable except he did catch it.

Jeremiah fought to control the mounting anger. This wasn't the first he'd heard this however… "I see. Tell me, Miss Lancaster, where is your family from?"

"The Lancasters? Well, here, in Albany, of course."

"I mean, originally? Because the original inhabitants were Indians." He'd let her mull that thought and he got the expected reaction of another shudder when he mentioned the natives to America.

"My family came from England, though we've been here for over a century. My grandfather fought in the War for Independence." She stood tall, pride clearly shining in her eyes.

"Miss Lancaster, perhaps you'd like to return to England. To your family's home."

She laughed. "Now, why on earth would I want to do that? New York is my home."

"Precisely. So why do you think I would want to return to Africa? Or any of the slaves? Because many of us have been here for generations and all we know is America. It is *our* home," he argued.

She stared at him with a confused look, as if he just told her the earth was flat and she was going to fall into the abyss.

"That seems hardly likely," she replied.

"To the contrary. I was a slave in Virginia, as was my mother and her mother before. All I have known or seen is this country. Why would I want to return to a land where I have no idea where my family was from? Hmmm?" His anger was slowly burning. How many Northern white people had thrown this stupidity at him and at Blacks in general? He knew that they pushed this versus having to deal with the 'freedmen' living next to them. As if they were sub-humans, the same argument the Southerners used for the continuation of slavery.

"But you hate America for slavery," she countered, her voice breaking some.

Behind her, he could see Larissa and Susan heading towards them with very determined looks on their faces. He wondered if they knew this woman was slowly aggravating him?

Allison's face lightened and she gave him a stunning smile. "I see the McHenry's calling me over. It was nice to meet you, Mr. Johnson." And she fluttered away toward the throng of white abolitionists near the food.

Thoroughly disgusted, he downed his glass of champagne in one gulp.

"Jeremiah, I've never seen you drink that much at one time," Larissa said once she reached his side.

"Yes, well, just another enlightening conversation with that woman."

"Miss Lancaster? Her father is a prominent lawyer in Albany. One we've been trying to win over to the cause," Susan stated.

"Maybe a lost attempt, if conversation with his daughter is any indication," Jeremiah snarled. "She's here for Thomas's sake, claiming to be his intended, but if that's the case, we are doomed if he becomes senator because she thinks all freedmen should return to Africa."

Larissa put her hand on his arm. "Relax. Thomas isn't likely to be drawn to that same conclusion."

"What makes you think so? She's just like many of the white people here, wanting us freed but gone. The question is, do you agree? Because if nothing else, Blacks, as slaves and freedmen, have built this country, with their backs, so we're more American citizens than many of the whites who dabble in this or that. We've sown our blood here, why should we leave?" He had to know. Was he fighting for freedom only for it to be shifted in getting rid of the Blacks?

"Jeremiah, no one says you have to leave. Only that small set that think they're greater than they are. Which," she darted a glance at Susan, "is precisely the reason we need to educate everyone on the matter."

"Most certainly," Susan agreed.

Larissa's confidence that all would be good with no deportations calmed him down for now. But he'd keep an eye on Miss Lancaster and if her relationship with Thomas would change him, because if that happened, it would be a disaster for them all.

*"Why, it's just like shooting squirrels, only these squirrels have guns, that's all."*
—Veteran of Fort Donelson rallying his Illinois farm boys. Battle of Shiloh, April 1862

# CHAPTER THIRTEEN

*Next morning*

Jaquita stretched, lounging just a moment longer in bed. Memories of last night swirling in her head, making her smile larger with every second. Her long kiss with Thomas McHenry played in her mind, as well as the touch of his body as he embraced her tightly. And his lips. Soft yet demanding, he'd kissed her hard and deeply, filling her soul with a longing she should avoid. When his lips traveled down her neckline, his tongue tracing a path, every nerve inside her lit on fire. Even now, the morning after, just the thought of what happened made her tingle with excitement. He'd kissed along her bodice neckline, slowly skating over the mounds of her breasts just above the fichu. The mere contact had made her nipples hard and her lower stomach light on fire.

Then, they'd stopped. He was panting, his eyes dark and wanting when he growled that they needed to return to the dance. She couldn't speak, her heart pounding so hard, she couldn't form the words and she was out of breath so she nodded as she put her hand on his arm to return to the dance floor.

The rest of the dance was a blur. She'd talked to a few others, danced with a couple but lost sight of him and that made her disappointed. She'd seen him bob in and out of the crowd but suddenly, he vanished. Without his presence, she deflated, exhausted and longing to leave. Bidding her hostess good night, she ran.

Now, though, she wondered if she'd see him again. Gripping the sheet beneath her as her hips swayed in a fashion she didn't understand, she forced herself to sit up and think straight. Thomas McHenry was a handsome man but she needed to remember that he was also a white man, and that white men rarely did anything worthy for a Black woman. Her basis for that way of thinking was simple. Her father. Pierre Fontaine claimed to her that he loved her mother, but her mother was a slave in his house and one he never freed to the best of her knowledge. So while he raised her with his white children, she feared his 'love' for her mother was nothing more than a lie to tell a mulatto child on the day her mama died.

She growled at that thought and slid out of bed. It was time to dress, and she was determined to spend her day forgetting the tall handsome lawyer. As she went down the stairs, she found a lovely array of flowers in the dining room with the scent of the lilies and roses filling the room. It was lovely, and she inhaled deeply.

Aunt Lila entered the room, carrying a tray to the table where she sat. Jaquita couldn't help but shake her head as the servant put the breakfast before her.

"One day, you'll tell me how you knew I was coming down for breakfast."

The house servant chuckled. "Some telltale signs and ways to do things never stop, Miss Jaquita."

"Thank you." She took a sip of the very hot coffee, being careful to go so to avoid burning her tongue. "The flowers are lovely. I don't recall the garden being in this advanced state."

"They were delivered this morning," Aunt Lila stated. "For you."

"Truly?" Her heart skipped a beat. "How grand! From who, did they tell you?"

The elder Black servant gave her a stern look, all most like a reprimand, Jaquita imagined. "From Mr. Thomas McHenry, III."

*He sent her flowers!* "They're so lovely." She bent to inhale one of the roses. Then she pulled the card next to the vase.

*To my favorite dancer, I hear you love to ride. I will collect you late*
   *morning and we will indulge in your love.*
   *Yours respectfully, T. McHenry, III*

She couldn't contain the squeal of excitement, though she caught Aunt Lila's glare out of the corner of her eye.

"You best mind your manners, missy. And don't go looking to attract any white man's attention. They're all full of mischief."

She did her best not to giggle too loudly yet lost. "I'll do my best." Inside, though, she jumped with joy.

Thomas sat regally on his horse, realizing he clutched the reins tighter than needed to be, as Jaquita settled into her sidesaddle, adjusting her skirts. He noted her riding outfit was a simple design of navy-blue wool with glass blue buttons and green piping. Her riding hat was black, the netting navy and the feather that draped down the back a mixture of black, blue and green. Surprisingly, the darker colors lightened her skin tones, which played in his head. She could almost pass for white and somehow, he figured, that would not make her happy.

"How did you hear of me riding?"

He smiled. "Your stable lad and mine are brothers."

Her eyes widened as she replied, "Oh, dear."

"Alex is a good lad. It was not bad tidings."

"I see," she stated, nudging her stallion to start walking. As they turned the corner at the end of the drive, she added, "What else did he say?"

"Oh, that you like to run fast." He winked. That motion set a myriad of emotions crossing her eyes, from what he could tell, and he watched in amazement in that split second from his comment to her grabbing her own reins tight, she was off like a lightning bolt down the dirt street. It made him steer his mount in the same direction, urging the gelding to kick into gear to reach her.

He chased her down the street and into the open greens beyond. His gelding matched her stallion in speed and then, when she caught his eye with a surprised look, he grinned and cut her horse off, turning them left. Even as the breeze roared past him, he could hear the faint echoes of her growl followed by the thunder of hooves as her mount kicked into high gear.

Over the dale they raced. He knew where he wanted to go and urged her to continue until he reached that point. The devil inside him was pushing him but how could he not? There was something about this woman he simply could not ignore.

As the raced down the worn path, the trees parted and a stream lay ahead. She was catching up and he knew it. The smile on his lips could not be contained as he pulled his horse up, despite the gelding's drive to win. With the stream so close, they both had to pull back hard on the reins before they found themselves in the middle of the water.

The horses snorted loudly, her stallion pawed the ground, his tail arched in a glorious array of black hair. Thomas noted the equine was of smaller stature, like he was built for a fragile beauty on his back. His dish face held an elegance Thomas hadn't seen, his movements like a dance. Whereas he'd expect a lady would have difficult with this agile animal, Jaquita kept her seat, her hands on the reins tight but not overly so as she *shhhhh'ed* him quietly, like a whisper. Her steed listened, as did Thomas's, and both horses soon stood, waiting for the next command.

"That is quite an animal," Thomas noted, sliding off his horse, dropping the reins and walking over to help her dismount.

"He is my pride and joy. He is an Arabian, one my father got years ago, and gave to me. His name is Maximus." She grinned broadly as she patted the stallion's withers.

"Maximus? Rather Roman name for an Arab horse."

She shrugged. "Aristotle seemed a bit too tame for him." She looked around. "Rather rude of you to cut me off, I'll have you know. And where are we?"

Thomas chuckled. "Perhaps but I wanted to come this way, and with you in the lead, I had a hard time telling you to turn."

She raised her eyebrows. "You started the race."

Hardly, he thought, but didn't say it. "We're actually in the northeast corner of the McHenry estates. My father bought a rather large land mass here and added on over the years. Rather cumbersome piece, one he planned to divide with his children. Alas, that's just me, so I have a rather immense green space."

"It's lovely." She peered over the greens. "Is that a house?"

"Yes. A vacant one. Guest house, really. A step maybe above plain. Originally the home to my grandmother when she was living. She tired of the mansion and wished for a cottage." He shrugged. "Haven't used it in years, though it is in good shape. I'd thought we'd have lunch there."

She was halfway to the door. "Wonderful. Riding makes me hungry."

He was hungry too, though his appetite wasn't for food…

The inside of the cottage was plain to someone like Thomas, she figured, but it was elaborate compared to the slave shanties in the South. The wood plank flooring was in the slave quarters at Bellefountaine home, though this one had a shine to it of polish and fitted snuggly together. The plastered walls were painted alabaster blue and the windows were more numerous than a slave's quarters and had real glass panes. The fireplace was tiled with ceramic pieces that had a floral design on them. The furniture in this cottage was maybe sparse but it was real, not like the makeshift pieces the slaves fabricated for theirs. All in all, she wanted to laugh at the white man's attempt to tell her how it was outdated or left vacant, indicating near nothing, but in her mind, when placed next to a Black man's house, it was grand. It was a difference even this lawyer who wanted slavery abolished would never understand.

A large wicker basket sat on the floor, near the fireplace. She noted the quilt on the floor for a 'picnic'. Slowly, she smiled. The thought that he had hoped she'd ride with him and be open to this sent a thrill up her spine.

"It's quite lovely. And I think you had a plan."

He laughed. "Perhaps. Here, let me take your wrap." Along with his frock coat, he placed her outer garments on the settee and then turned to the basket. With a whisk, he pulled out a bottle of wine.

"So why would you seek my company?" She couldn't help the words, despite her inner voice telling her to be quiet and enjoy the repast. "I mean, this is all very grand, but don't you have a job to do?"

The cork popped out and he chuckled again. "I do have a few law cases to work on and a steady, planned agenda for most of my life. It can be rather dull and boring. Then I met you. A beautiful and vivacious woman who pushes for rights that she expects are hers and doesn't let the others win. That lioness part of you attracted me from the moment I first met you." He handed her a glass of the ruby red wine. "A woman I wanted to know."

She took a sip. It was exquisite. "New York is filled with many ladies who could offer you the same desire. Ones more acceptable for you to seek."

"Ah, but that's the reason. I don't search for acceptable. I want *real*." He took her wine glass and set it aside, pulling her into his arms and kissed her.

Jaquita wasn't expecting this. But the moment he invaded her lips, she knew at once that same desire he was explaining. She slipped her arms around his neck and returned his kiss in full. It was heady and she drank him in, pressing herself against him.

He broke from her lips and started to kiss her jawline, back toward one ear, his teeth skating along her skin. His touch started a fire inside her, making every nerve alive and pulsing insanely. One hand came to undo the buttons on her bodice and when she realized that was what he was up to, she had to help. She couldn't breathe with it all cinched up, and she was so hot, she feared she'd faint. As the bodice opened, he shoved it off her shoulders, freeing her of the piece as he resumed kissing her neckline.

The riding outfit was one piece and with the bodice hanging off her back, the weight of the wool increased. Or perhaps that really was from his fiery kisses. And then instantly, the weight dropped as he undid the hook at her waist and the dress fell without the crinoline to keep it up. Only her corded petticoat remained of her skirting. leaving Jaquita in her undergarments before a dressed man. Her thoughts jumbled when her inner voice screamed that would not do!

To correct the balance between them, she pulled back and started undoing his waistcoat. A glance at his eyes revealed everything. His blue eyes looked black and hooded and his whole body was rigid. She couldn't help but grin, despite her racing blood.

"You, dear sir, are overly attired."

Quickly, he joined her in undoing the buttons and the waistcoat and then his necktie and shirt all sailed to the floor. But when her fingers went to his trousers, he grabbed them to stop.

"My dearest Jaquita, we are now treading on grounds over which we may regret going." His voice held a deep and husky tone, a delicious sound that made her insides molten.

"You're telling me now that you do not want me?" She was confused. Her body was now a furnace and only his attention could cool it, yet he didn't want to?

He laughed, pulling her tight against him. "Oh yes, I do. And badly." He kissed her hard, like a man on fire, devouring her.

He lowered them to the floor, on top of the blanket. With a hard push, the basket tumbled out of their way. She couldn't help but smile as he loomed over her, his fingers tracing the top of her chemise.

"Now is the time to stop me or be forever mine."

*"As to disunion, nobody but silly people believe it will happen."*

—William Cullen Bryant, The New York editor, echoing the majority of Republicans feelings post the 1860 election.

# CHAPTER FOURTEEN

He wanted her to stop him. Was on the verge of begging her to. But she lay beneath him, frocked in white cotton undergarments, breathing heavily so her breasts pushed against the corset and the mounds peeking above the chemise made the wolf inside him growl with hunger. He wanted her badly and his manhood throbbed so hard, if she said no, he'd probably die in pain.

Instead, her hand slipped around his neck and cupped the back of his head, pulling him back down to kiss her again and all was lost. He bathed her in kisses and small bites on her neck. Within seconds, he untied the cord at her waist, undid the busk to her corset freeing her, and unbuttoned waistband to the corded petticoat, pushing it down over her hips to free her of the contraption around her waist. He continued kissing her as he pulled the chemise up over her head to toss the piece aside and exposed her naked upper body to him. Her pearled nipples called to him, the mounded flesh beneath glowed and the narrow waist hinted at the delights below still covered in the loose petticoat. He wasted no time in shedding that off her, exposing her whole being, wearing only black cotton stockings and black riding boots.

She was a dark Aphrodite and he was totally under her spell. "You are so beautiful."

Her cheeks pinkened and the glow over her made his insides tighten harder. He pulled her into his arms and kissed her. But she didn't just return his kiss. Her nimble fingers started on his drawers' buttons and when her fingertips skated over his manhood, he nearly exploded. Quickly, he flipped them back over so she was back on her back and he pulled up, trying to keep her eyes on him. Of course, that didn't work. They looked down at his hardened member. He feared she'd withdraw because he knew he was in pain from the erection and that'd turn it red.

Instead, she gave him a half smile with a wink and wrapped her hand around him. The feel of her on his cock nearly sent him over the edge. "Be careful, darling."

"I will," she cooed. Then she gasped when he found her core and slipped his finger in. Instinctively, her thighs parted more and her hips tipped back. She was wet and open and he couldn't help it. He poised the head of his cock at her slit and stopped.

"I want you." It was a rasp, he knew, but this

wasn't the time to regret joining with her.

Her hazel eyes were dark brown with desire. Placing her hands on his hips, she pulled him into her. She was wet but tight and as he pushed deeper, she yelped. To get past her virginal seal, he thrust all the way as his mouth encased hers to swallow her scream. He stopped and gave her the moment to adjust. When he felt her squirm a tad, he began to move.

In and out they danced, hips meeting then separating. It was languorous at first until the need took control. The faster they moved, deeper he went. She mewled when he pulled back and he moaned when he slid back in. The heat between them skyrocketed and so did their desire. Her nails dug into his back and he relished every ounce of the pain they caused. Over and over and over they melded and pulled back until her core tightened so tight around him, he plunged in and exploded his seed inside of her right as he felt her core shatter.

Completed, he collapsed on top of her, gasping for air. It was jubilant, ecstasy and within a minute, he feared he'd made a big mistake.

Jaquita couldn't breathe. Her whole world had exploded into stars in her head when she released. The entire lovemaking had been so bright and fulfilling. Now she understood why parents protected their daughters and it made her want to laugh and cry, because as a mulatto child, not free but not slaved, she wasn't protected. It was an odd feeling but she decided to toss it aside for now.

"Are you all right?" he asked quietly.

She winced. "Yes. Perhaps a bit sore."

"Sorry about that. You'll be worse later." He kissed her lips in a chaste kiss and rolled away, collecting his clothes.

She perched herself up off the blanket, watching him pull his drawers back up. "I'm still hungry."

He stopped and gave her an odd smile with a half laugh. "We will eat and then return." He tossed her the chemise. "Perhaps we should dress. Catching a cold from prancing in our birthing suits might cause talk."

She raised her brows. "I guess you're right."

They dressed and quickly devoured the bread and cheese he had brought. The wine didn't last long either.

As she re-pinned her hair, thankful that she could pile most of it up under the crown of her hat, she cast him a slanted gaze.

"You regret what we did."

He was picking up their dishes and stopped. In a moment, he was at her side, taking her in his arms and kissed her so deeply, she couldn't breathe and was crushed by his tight embrace.

"Now, does that answer your question?"

*Men!*

*3 Days Later*

Thomas yawned. He was too tired to think law so he threw the papers he'd been trying to read back on his desk and rubbed his eyes. The reason for his exhaustion wasn't work but Jaquita. Since their ride and lovemaking, he was caught in her spell. After that day, he tried to stay away from her, because what good would come of it? He was a white lawyer, hopefully a senator where he could push the abolition of slavery through as law. But she was colored and came from the South. He'd look no better than any slave owner taking advantage of his chattel and that thought made his blood boil.

Memories of her laughter, of how she made him smile, of her determination and how beautiful she was flooded his mind and before he knew it, he was back calling on her. They'd gone to lunch, to dinner, to shop, for long walks and it was only three days! He shook his head, feeling like he was on the road, but which way? Hell or Heaven?

"Knock, knock."

Thomas blinked and looked up. It was Frederick and he had a strange look on his face.

"Come in. What is wrong?"

"Who said anything was wrong?" the tall German Anglo asked, plopping himself down in the leather-bound chair on the other side of the desk.

"The look on your face."

"Ah, yes, well, you haven't been here when we needed to be discussing your campaign."

Thomas leaned back in his chair, narrowing his gaze. "I thought you were handling that."

"Yes, and you need to be involved. Word has it no one has heard a peep out of you since that abolitionist fundraiser you attended."

"I have been busy. I do work, you know." Frankly, he had forgotten about the election.

"Yes, and I've also been told of a certain lady you've been keeping time with. A lovely, but Black, lady. A Miss Fontaine." Frederick glared. "Look, I understand playing the abolitionist hand is noteworthy, but not at exclusion of everything else."

"Her family has money," he tried. "Donations would be a benefit."

"Her 'family' are Southerners. Doubtful they'd send money for a Northern senator running with a platform to eliminate their 'chattel'."

Thomas's jaw tightened. "I enjoy her company."

"All well and good and even from a political standpoint, of being for freeing the slaves, perhaps commendable, however," Frederick argued. "As a bachelor, you need a wife more compatible to today's voters, like Miss Lancaster. I've heard word you've been sighted with her on occasion."

Inwardly, Thomas cringed. Allison. "Yes, she was at that abolitionist ball with me." Well, he met her there. She'd come to surprise him and she sure did. It put a damper on his evening as he couldn't see Jaquita again before the night was through with her tagging along with him.

"Your father has hinted at a hidden romance there. If I were you, and she willing, that would be an ideal candidate. Her family is wealthy and a great influence in the area." Frederick smiled smugly, sitting back in his chair.

Thomas wanted to roll his eyes but refrained. Yes, his father had suggested her as well on repeated times. Despite her being pleasant, even attractive, Allison was also too forward and demanding. How could he marry her when his heart called for Jaquita? And almost on cue, there was another knock at his opened door.

"Thomas, good afternoon!" Allison greeted, then saw Frederick. "I hope I'm not intruding. My father had an appointment with your father, so I thought I'd stop in to say hello."

Frederick stood, his grin now firmly set on his face, making Thomas long to slap it off. "No, my good lady, I was just leaving." He grabbed his hat and shot Thomas a look. "Give it some consideration. It'd win you votes."

"I certainly will," he answered with mocking sincerity. He could hear Frederick laugh as he walked down the corridor. With a shake of his head, he forced the conversation aside and rose with a smile.

"Miss Lancaster, what a pleasure."

*"I appear this evening as a thief and robber. I stole this head, these limbs, this body from my master, and ran off with them."*

—Frederick Douglass, son of a slave and a white man, ran away twice from his owner. Eloquent speaker, accused of never being a slave, he raised $600 from English admirers to buy his freedom.

# CHAPTER FIFTEEN

Jaquita let her body soak in the tub just a moment longer. The water was cooling, despite it being near the fireplace, but her muscles were sore from riding and working in her garden. No, she smiled. Maybe that wasn't the reason, but a certain man was. A trill spun down her spine, pooling in her loins at the thought. Thomas. She sighed.

He was a man of many desires. They had shopped, ate, rode, went on a boat ride, played billiards as well as croquet and danced. The last two weeks had been a whirlwind of fun, many times ending with them entangled in an intimate dance with memories that made her thankful she was in a tub of water so if her hips moved, it was well hidden.

He'd also sent her notes. Mostly short, many

just with comments on how he loved his time with her and when he hoped to see her again. Every one excited her, every moment leading her heart deeply down a path she wasn't sure she wanted but by now, was a foregone conclusion— she was falling in love with him.

That realization made her heart skip a beat and a wave of cold wash over her. Deciding that was the water's temperature and not fear, she reached for her linen sheet and got out of the tub. It took no time to dry, dress and do her hair for her to be out the door. She'd deal with her emotions later. Now, she had errands to do.

Thomas shook his head again, trying desperately not to nod off asleep. The last week had exhausted him. The campaign for senate had eaten time, work stole what it could and Frederick's advice was applied. In the last ten days, he'd escorted Allison to two social affairs, where he made numerous political contacts, took her for a carriage ride and a dance at the city hall. It was the only night he hadn't seen Jaquita, since the other events were during the day. So seeing his lover at night and courting a lady for political reasons started to take its toll. Every time he was with Jaquita, he wanted to strangle Frederick for his comments about marriage. And when he was with Allison, he could see they'd be an amiable match, what many upper-class New Yorkers had.

It boiled down to which did he want? A pretty white wife, whose family was stable, strong New

Yorkers with wealth and contacts? Or a Black wife, a bastard out of a Southern slave family, whose father acknowledged her but was also against the Northern view on slavery, and the one lady he loved? He just might go insane.

"Thomas!"

Thomas frowned. His father. "Here!" Though the thought of jumping out the window did cross his mind.

Thomas McHenry II breezed into his son's office with a wide grin on his face. "Congratulations, my boy! I just heard of your engagement! Bravo!"

Yes, he inwardly groaned. He'd seen it on the gossip rag this morning. "Thank you, I guess."

His father poured them a drink but shot his son a discerning look at his reply. "Never guess, dear boy. For your political future and the future of the McHenry family, you have made a solid and well thought out decision. The Lancasters are very influential and they like you. Half the game is done!" He shoved a drink into Thomas's hand and then clanged it with his as a toast. "To the future Senator McHenry!"

As his father downed the drink, Thomas stared at the glass, absently wondering if Jaquita viewed the newsprints and prayed she didn't....

Jaquita finished dressing, her grin and good mood never leaving her. She put the final hair comb into place and left her room to head downstairs when she ran into Clarence at the foot of the stairs.

"A visitor, ma'am."

She nodded and headed toward the front parlor to find Jeremiah there with a brooding look on his face. He always seemed to be dire, she decided.

"Jeremiah, what a pleasant surprise! You barely caught me before I left for the night."

"Yes, well I think you might want to rethink your plans." His tone sounded ominous.

"Whatever do you mean?"

"You've been seeing that lawyer, haven't you? Thomas McHenry?" He stood at the fireplace, the look of a master from down South etched in his face, as if he caught her trying to run away or such. Ice dripped down her spine.

"That's a rather forward and uncalled for question, as if I did something wrong."

"Just answer it, Jaquita."

She frowned. He was so serious. "Yes, I have accompanied Mr. McHenry about town. Why?"

"Yes, well, have you seen the newspapers?"

She noticed he had one rolled in his hand. "No."

"Well your appearances with him did set the gossips to goin'," he mumbled, walking to the table in front of the settee and spreading out the papers. "See?"

She glanced. It was a drawn picture of them at the millinery shop three days past. "Not a bad likeness. We were looking at a new hat for him." She laughed. "I don't understand why you seem so upset."

"You realize, the abolitionist movement is growing here in the North. People are starting to see the abomination of slavery and joining our ranks to see it overturned. But despite all that, even here in free New York, people frown on mixed relationships."

"That is ridiculous! I've seen other mixed couples—"

"Where?" His face was tinged red. "The Irish will mix with us, well, some of the Irish lasses, and their men hate it. We are still below their societal ranks, and barely tolerated."

"That will change, I am sure," she said with a determined voice, one that even surprised her. Perhaps Thomas was the source of that pride.

"But not in our lifetime!" He started to pace. "I only bring this to your attention to save you."

"Save me?" Her brows furrowed as she glared at him.

He grabbed the corner of the page and turned it, pointing to the top. It was a page marked *Wedding Announcements* and below that headline, under *Engagements*, she found an equally good drawing of Thomas—with another woman, with the latest on their engagement. Her jaw dropped open.

"Allison Lancaster is from a rather rich family here. Her father is a lawyer turned politician, a senator, no less," he stated. "A marriage that'd advance Mr. McHenry's run for office immensely."

She couldn't breathe. Her heart plummeted. He'd betrayed her. She blinked hard when her vision started to blur. Tears started to escape and that only increased her burning anger. "No," was all she could whisper.

"I see, so it was more than a casual outing," he snarled. "Jaquita, don't you see? He's no better than the slaveowners down South!" A southern drawl she didn't know he had started to uncurl in his speech. "He took advantage of you 'cause he could! Tell me, did he ever offer to marry you? And what if you're with his child, huh? What then? Send you off to some mammy down South to rid yourself of it? Or pay you off to leave? Bastard!"

Inside she started to shake. Pregnancy. She didn't have to worry on that as her flow came last week. But what he said had truth. Thomas never talked of a future with her. It hadn't bothered her then but now? A look at the paper told her as of now, that'd never happen.

"Jeremiah, thank you for showing me the error of my ways. If you don't mind, please leave. I need some time alone." She was a shattered mess, her heart cracking and she refused to cry any further.

Jeremiah took her hands in his and squeezed. "I'm so sorry, Jaquita. But I thought you needed to know. I'm here if you need me." And he left.

Jaquita sank to the settee, her back rigid straight as her stomach flipped. *What was she to do, now that her heart was broke in two?*

*Livingston Ball*

Thomas downed another champagne glass, praying for something stronger, but still had the sense not to ask for it. He wasn't sure he ever felt this alone before in his life. Plenty of times he wanted to be left alone, yet in a room filled with guests milling about, it was an odd sensation to feel that way now.

The Livingston Ball was one of the fetes of the season and it was the ideal place for a candidate for office to be seen. It was also the ideal place for a couple to announce their engagement. He had escorted Allison here, and without a doubt, he was sure she thought that this was where they'd formally announce theirs. Damn, he needed another glass! Maybe another would drown the vision of Jaquita from his mind, of her spinning with him on the dance floor, of her light and airy laughter and the fire she stoked in him when they made love. How was he to ever put that aside for Allison? The Lancaster girl was sweet, pretty and so well mannered, though time consuming, he severely tired of her. He had yet to kiss her, mostly because he had no desire to, and that told him more than he wanted to know.

"Thomas! There you are!" Frederick sauntered up. "Thought you'd be out on the floor with the soon-to-be bride, or imbibing with the power players."

"I needed a break," he confided. "This campaigning is tiring. Thought you were doing all the ground work for me, the stumping as it were."

"Dear man, I am! Now it is your turn for them to hear your voice." He nudged Thomas in the arm in jest.

The crowd started a louder mumble and many turned to look at the main doorway to the dance floor. Their mood swing caught Thomas's attention and he followed them to find another arrival, a tad late, and therefore even more dramatic. At the doorway stood that abolitionist, Jeremiah Johnson, and on his arm was Jaquita.

Thomas stood stunned. She looked gorgeous. Dressed in a blue silk dress with cream lace and black trim, her hair a mass of curls, most of which was piled on her head with a few escaping confinement. She took his breath away.

As Jeremiah nodded to the announcement of their arrival, she scanned the room and found him. He was too far to tell her expression but all he wanted was to be with her. He was doomed. Doomed or not, he put his glass down and started in her direction.

"Thomas," Frederick warned, in a low tone, as he quickly caught up. "You need to watch your steps. All the room will watch as well."

He smiled at a couple of the attendees as he past them. The string quartet was starting to count to the beginning of the next dance and he'd be the first on her list, he swore!

"Don't worry so much. Talking to Jeremiah is nothing but positive in this game of politics," he replied and strode a bit quicker, maneuvering through people to get to them by the time they got past the host and hostess.

"My lady Jaquita, what a pleasant surprise to see you," he murmured, taking her gloved hand and kissing it. Her dance card bobbed off that wrist and he swore she swung it so it hit him near his eye. He half-smiled. She was still alive!

"May I have the honor of this dance?" he asked. She gave him a puzzled look and started to open her mouth but her expression had turned sour, so he grabbed her hand more firmly and directed her away with him. "Lovely. I'm honored."

He spun her in front of him out on the dance floor and now saw the fire in her eyes.

"I did not say I'd dance with you."

"True, but why would you not?" He smiled. She still didn't.

As the music started, he bowed to her curtsey and then put a hand on her waist and took the other. It was a waltz, and he couldn't think of a better dance to have with her. As they started around the floor, he realized she wouldn't look at him and felt stiff in his arms. He rolled his lips in, fearing she'd read the paper on his engagement and he felt pain like she gut punched him for it.

"Jaquita—"

"No, Thomas, no," she cut him off, finally glaring darts at him. "Just as well we are dancing, so I can tell you I never want to see you again. How dare you!"

"It's not what you think."

"How would you know what I think? You spend time with me, make me laugh, show me how wonderful love can be, only to find that you'll marry another? I'd spit at you, but we are in a public place. And as it is, being Black, I have limited rights, it appears."

"You have it wrong," he started. How could he

show her it wasn't her fault?

"You took advantage of me," she hissed. "Jus' lika massa does his slave!" Her slur into the white man's world of how slaves talked and what they endured hit him like a sledgehammer.

"I did not take advantage of you. You enjoyed it just like I did. But I'm running for office—"

"Yes, I heard, and there, Black wives are forbidden!" Luckily the music was loud enough, he doubted anyone else heard them but now, it was the final notes and they all stopped.

"Jaquita, please—"

The dancers all clapped except her. She gave him an icy, stabbing glance and spun on her slipper, heading straight off the floor without him.

Allison took another sip of her champagne, vaguely listening to her mother's neighbor ramble on something as she watched her future husband take that woman out onto the dance floor. Now, Allison knew she'd won him fair and square as her spouse, but what was this all about? She saw them twirl in a very awkward way and the mulatto woman refused to look at him till the end. Whatever she spouted, Allison couldn't hear, but when she sped away from him at the end of the dance, she wanted to dance in celebration. Oh, she'd seen the gossip on them and worried, only marginally, that he cared for the girl more than his future wife, but if the way this dance ended meant anything, Allison had nothing to worry about. She grinned.

As he walked up to her, she met him part way. "Hello, stranger."

He chuckled. "Sorry. Politics. Here," he offered her his arm and she gladly accepted.

His buddy Frederick called them over. He stood with a group of men, including her father. She forced the smile to stay on her face despite the fact she'd bet the conversation would be on politics. At least they wouldn't have the gall to mention *that* woman being here.

"Our dear future senator, how does it feel to be out with all who support you?" her father asked.

"Senator Lancaster, it still takes a bit to get used to."

The cluster laughed.

"I see your fellow abolitionists arrived. Always a pleasure to add a little 'color' to our events," Mr. Clothworthy added. Allison nodded along with the rest, except for Thomas.

"Perhaps that's a bit harsh," Frederick interjected. Allison bet it was to cut Thomas off from saying something that might not sit well. His support of the cause was one of his platforms.

"They're just as good to be here as we are," Thomas said.

"Yes, but they can't vote," Clothworthy added.

"The abolitionists are working on that, as are the suffragists," Thomas argued.

"Oh, don't bring those creatures up!" another man hissed. "I'd rather give the freedmen the right to vote over women." He looked at Allison and added, "Apologies, no offense given."

She nodded, though the thought irritated her. *Give it to the coloreds and not women?*

"Well, let's get slavery abolished first and vote next," Thomas suggested.

"Here, here," several of the men said.

"Slavery is awful," Allison said, finding her voice. She needed to support her future husband.

"They all need to be freed and now! And those slave-owners need to give them money, too," one of the group said. All applauded.

"But where are they going to go? They won't stay South but do we want them all up here?" Clothworthy asked. Half the group shook their head.

"That is part of freedom, gentlemen and lady," Thomas answered. "To decide where they want to live."

"Don't you think they'd rather go home?" Allison queried. "Back to their ancestral home? Africa? They were stolen from there. I think we should return them at no cost to them."

She got hurrahs from part of the group but Thomas stared at her as if she'd asked for wings to fly.

"Most have been here for generations," he answered. "This country is their home."

"I doubt any of those buggers would call the place that enslaved them home," one of the men to the right added.

"Narrow minded view there, Fitzpatrick," Frederick proclaimed. "But you're Irish. I get that. Would you like it if we sent you back to Ireland?"

"My folks wanted to leave Ireland, plague and all. Why would I want to return?"

"Exactly." Clothworthy.

"Well, I think we should send them home." Allison smiled. In her mind, it was the perfect solution. "I mean, do you want them to live next to you? Their children with yours in school? Go to the same church?" She shuddered. "They'd have their place in Africa."

Thomas just stared at her, as if she were a creature in the zoo. "Well, don't you agree, darling?" she asked him.

Thomas rolled his bottom lip in, a strange look in his eye. "Gentlemen, if you'll excuse us." He offered her his arm and she thankfully took it. Politics bored her immensely!

As they walked away, he led her toward the front and requested her cloak.

"We're leaving? It's a bit early."

"Yes, you are leaving and so am I," he answered, putting her wrap around her and taking his overcoat. "I will drop you by home and that will be it, Allison."

"It? What do you mean?" He seemed so strange she was confused.

Buttoning his overcoat, he said, "You'd send the freedmen to what you think is their home, because you don't want to live near them?"

"Well, no. Surely you don't either."

He gave her a queer smile and tied her bonnet for her. "I see no problem with them here. They are people, like you and me. After they've been enslaved and dictated to for generations, we owe them the right to make their own choices."

"In Africa!" she demanded.

"Here," he rebutted.

Horrified at the thought of his future, she felt like a rock fell into her stomach. "We can't do this. I can't marry a man who will do nothing to protect me."

"Excuse me?"

"Well, as you state, they've been abused all this time. How do you know they won't take it out on us? On white people? I could be violated, in revenge for those Southern owners raping their women! Or stealing from us because we have more. No, no, they have to go!" She started to shake. The mere thought of them taking revenge made her blood race and her head hurt.

He took her arm and walked her out to the carriage. "You are panicking over something that isn't true."

"How do you know!?" she screeched, her mind flooded with fear.

"I'll go get your mother. Sam!" he called to the driver. "Wait here till I get Mrs. Lancaster." He helped her into vehicle and then closed the door. "Good bye, Miss Lancaster."

She watched him walk away and frowned. That was too formal a good bye from a fiancé...

*"All the indications are that this treasonable inflammation—secessionitis—keeps on making steady progress, week by week."*
—George Templeton Strong, Wall Street attorney, 1861

# CHAPTER SIXTEEN

Thomas's stomach flipped. He could *not* marry that woman! What she argued and feared was his worst nightmare. Her fears were unfounded to his way of thinking. Allison might be the right political move, but she didn't support his beliefs that slavery should be abolished, not the way he believed in them. And her attack on the poor souls who'd already had their lives stolen was uncalled for. He could not live with that type of person and the thought of intimacy with someone who was so singularly minded was out of the question.

He raced in, got her mother and told her that Allison had had a sick spell and needed to leave. Then he found Frederick. The campaign manager only confirmed his disbelief over her outrage, telling him she'd said this before. He closed his eyes in anger, wanting to explode. All this garbage over social standing and the election had made him make the wrong decision. He loved another woman and now, she hated him.

By the time he realized what he'd done, he was in a carriage stopped before Jaquita's house. He stared at the front door, debating with himself. What could he say to win her back? She'd thrown strong barbs at him, entirely justified he knew. Would she take an apology? Was she even home?

At the door, the elderly butler let him in. The man was good at his job, with no indication in his face what he felt. Good for him, bad for Thomas. Now he stood in the front parlor, pacing. It took him a moment to realize she was standing in the doorway, leaning against the framing in the same ball gown, one eyebrow raised questioning him.

"This had better be good," she stated flatly. "Before I have you thrown out."

"I came to apologize," he started, walking toward her. "I was an ass. I allowed myself to believe others, instead of believing myself." He took her hand, stunned she'd let him but her skin was ice cold and motionless. Visions of previous lectures by former slaves came to mind, of having to submit even when angry, because the master had the right. He squeezed her hand, looking for a response and still, nothing.

"I did propose to Miss Lancaster. But I did not love her. I didn't even want her, but her connections would help me in my election and that was my sin. To push for my own self-interests, even if I saw my main motivation was you and to help your people. At any rate, she showed her true colors tonight, how she wasn't in the fight with me as I needed, and it hit me like a lightning bolt that the one person who understood, the one I love, now hated me." He bent down on one knee and looked up into her eyes. "Please forgive this wretched soul."

She returned his look but he couldn't read her. She was still, like a statue. He feared all was lost when she suddenly laughed.

"Wretched soul? Oh, that was good." She covered her mouth and laughed into her hand.

He smiled, then frowned, still unsure as he slowly rose. "Will you forgive me?"

"You left Miss Perfect to come here with some concocted tale to 'beg' for my forgiveness?"

"I left her. Period. I can't marry her. I might lose the election, but I'm still a good lawyer and can still push for anti-slavery in other ways." He was drowning and she wasn't saving him. "Please forgive my obstinacy, for believing the idiots around me."

"So that's it? Nothing with Miss Fancy-Clothes?"

Now he laughed. "No. Told her father I couldn't. She was too confused to understand when I said good bye, I meant it."

Her mouth twisted. She pulled her hand from his and stepped back. "I don't know Thomas. I gave you all I am and you threw me aside for a political, and a social, bias. How am I to know that you won't change your mind and take her back? Or find one more agreeable to your itinerary?"

"Hmmmmm," he started, now pacing with her. "Perhaps, you're right. I have found another, one who has the fight in her. I mean, who else comes to a fashionable and wildly attended ball to take me down a notch and leave? You!"

"Nice, but—"

He tired of her words and pulled her close, descending on her lips in one fell swoop kiss. Hard, demanding and met with equal demands, he devoured her. Until she ripped herself out of his embrace.

"No! No! Aunt Lila was right. You white boys are just all full of mischief! Thinking you can kiss your way back into my good graces, until another throws at you that mixed relationships are not acceptable! So how dare you even try!"

Thomas ground his teeth. "I'm not like that."

"Ha! But you are!" She was fuming and he deserved it. "How about how I feel? Had you considered that?"

He dropped to one knee again, taking her hand. In his pocket was the engagement ring he was to present to Allison tonight at the dance, though he didn't want to. He'd picked it out with Jaquita in mind, over two months ago, so he just couldn't give it to Allison. It took arguing with himself to think to do so tonight, tied to her, but now, a part of him jumped with joy to give it to the woman who it was bought for. He pulled it out of his pocket and taking her hand, started to put it on.

"Jaquita Fontaine, will you marry me? I truly love you."

He got the ring on and the diamond sparkled. It looked glorious. He glanced at her, praying.

Her response was fast. *Slap!*

*1863*

Jaquita played with her gloves as they sat in the
carriage on their way home. Her mind was
still troubled and anger brewing. She glared out
the window, feeling the fire inside her flicker
brighter than it had in a while.

"Must have been a sight to see your brother
this evening," Thomas started. "He's not the one
who is in the Union Army, right?"

She tugged her bottom lip in, aggravation on
the rise. "No. It was Francois, my oldest brother."
She snorted. "Rather a surprise he joined the fray.
He told me he was one of the Louisiana Tigers."

"That's fierce group. How'd he get up here?"

She looked out the window and sighed. "He
was with Ada Lorrance. You recall her from the
Abolition Society?"

"Ah, yes, that woman doctor. Heard she'd gone
to help the Union Army, though how, not sure.
They don't believe women doctors qualify to
practice on men."

"Think she said she went in as a nurse.
Apparently, Francois has a foot wound and she's
tending him." The irony of the scenario still
slayed her. "Considering Francois's penchant for
colored women, and as a slave owner, to be under
the care of a stalwart abolitionist has got to be
quite a relationship!"

He chuckled.

Then the silence returned. She didn't have to put up with it too long as they pulled up in front of their mansion. He quickly got out and lifted her down but she pulled free and stormed up the stairs. Each clop of her heels on the cement stairs to the front door echoed her anger. She knew he wasn't right behind, meaning he knew she was mad. The fact that he hadn't said a word was only fueling her anger.

Once in the parlor and she heard him enter, she spun. "We are a joke."

He gave her a frown as he walked to the sideboard and pulled a glass. "That's a bit severe. How so?"

*He was so dense!* "When are you finally going to make me an honest woman and not your live-in whore?!"

Thomas had the bourbon bottle in his hand, ready to pour into a glass when she sent that accusation at him. Inwardly, he groaned. He should have expected this. So why did it surprise him now?

"Jaquita, please," he begged, finishing pouring his glass.

"No, do not start that! You're in office. They've all seen us together. Heavens, we live together, despite you maintaining I live here and you at your house! How long do you intend to play this farce?" She was livid. He knew that.

"Most of them already assume we are married."

"But we are not and you know that! Fix it,

Senator!" She stormed up to him, her cheeks fire red. "Fix it or you're leaving here. Tonight!"

"You're pushing the acceptance level. You know as much as the North wants slavery abolished, mixed marriage isn't truly accepted."

She slapped his face hard. "You proposed to me six years ago! It was my mistake to say yes, apparently, because you have managed to put it off over and over again," she fumed. "One hour. I give you one hour to pack your bags and leave my life forever!"

She virtually ran to the door. He had to stop her.

"And what of Tommy?" he roared.

She stopped but didn't turn around. "I'm perfectly able to raise our son without you. Remember, I come from a family with money."

"Ha! There's a war and they are the enemy! Answer me that!"

She turned and gave him a sinister look. Those eyes. They could see right through him.

"And you think all their assets are in the South?" She left.

Angry, he threw the glass at the fireplace and thank God he'd downed its contents because the drops in it set the fire to blaze.

Clarence appeared as if out of the air, surprising Thomas, though at this point, so many years here, it wasn't as if this was new.

"Sir, if you'll move, I can clean the area a bit."

Thomas saw the glass shards near the fireplace and fire had reduced to the minimal flames. He moved.

"Tell me, Clarence, how long does her anger hold? I should know this, but she's never gotten this upset."

The elderly servant moved with a methodical pattern with the broom and pan. "Well, sir, ain't my place to say."

"Indulge me, please."

He stopped and stood, looking at Thomas straight on. The elderly butler himself looked red as if anger, or maybe from the heat of the blaze still resonating in the room.

"Sir, that girl loves you. You've known that. You have an amazing child. And he's light enough, could almost pass for white. However, you've left her on a string and that boy's inheritance in jeopardy by refusing to marry her."

He stood, shaking his head. "I'm a politician. I need to steer this land via laws towards freeing the slaves. We're at war over this. As much as I want to claim her legally, it could cost me my position in Congress." He sat, discouraged. Mixed marriages were frowned on, despite the urge for abolition. To him, it shouldn't matter…

"Sir, if you don't mind me asking, what is she to you?"

Puzzled, Thomas looked at him and replied, "She's the woman I love."

He nodded, taking his time with placing the dust pan. His quiet ate at Thomas's nerves, because the lawyer knew he had more to say.

"Well, sir, love is good and all," the butler started. "Down South, women folk hear that all the time from men not wanting to commit or anything."

"I'm not avoiding commitment. Look all around you. We live together. She's called Mrs. McHenry. If I didn't want that, well," he stopped, hearing his own words. Silence fell as he felt his world starting to crumble. After a minute, he added, "It's just not that easy."

"I see," the older man mumbled, sweeping the area.

Aggravated, he started to pace. "She's the woman I want to spend my life with."

"I see." He brushed more of the glass into the pan. "How long you wanna be in politics?"

Still blazing a trail in the floor, he spat, "God, not any longer than I have to be!"

The butler stopped and gave him a low grin. "Then what's in your way?"

Thomas startled. Damn, he hated to think it, but the man was right. He loved Jaquita and his time in Congress wasn't forever. So he'd lose her for his own stupidity? Oh, hell no!

"Thanks Clarence!" And he raced out the door and out of the house.

Jaquita peeked in on her son and found the toddler curled up in his bed, deep asleep. She smiled and envied his escape from this world. Silently, she left and went to her room, yanking her carpetbag out of the armoire. She didn't want Thomas to leave, but she couldn't continue this way. Ada had introduced her to her brother as Jaquita McHenry, and to most of Washington, she had been called that. What was his problem with making it happen?

To her, it all boiled down to one thing. He didn't truly love her. The whole set up was a farce, since they still had the two homes but she was to stay here and not move in his. No better than any master/slave relationship. That analogy made her stomach flip, though a laugh escaped her mouth. Thomas had listened when she told him of her family, of how she had grown up as part of the family and not at the same time. How her father reminded her he had loved her mother and how he seemed to smooth over the prickling heat she caught from his white wife for having a 'slave child' in with her brood. Thomas had listened and asked her questions that she now knew were pointed ones, pulling out the sordid shadows she had carefully tucked away. Little nuisances of how, despite his affirmation of affections, Pierre Fontaine had never freed her mother, never letting her have the chance to deny him. And that had descended on Jaquita, for she had believed him and never truly considered her situation was that bad since she had the education her white siblings had and access to finer things, though in reality, Pierre had smothered her lies, promising in unspoken words that he loved his mulatto daughter, while the sins of the Fontaine family exploded around her. Of mixed-race children not as fortunate as her and how the slave life surrounding her was hell. Thomas had brought the truth to her eyes and she hated him for it, crying buckets as the white walls crumbled to the ground.

Then, as she fell to a heap on the floor, he had picked her up in his arms, holding steadfastly as her outrage settled to just glowing embers. He'd helped her see her past in clear sight, and for that, she fell deeper in love with him. She threw herself into the abolitionist society with all her might, with him at her side. It was heaven. But it was one that was only a veil of what it could be as their false 'engagement' lagged on, not hitting home until she saw Francois tonight of just how much time she had wasted, on a man who did exactly what her father had done, whispering promises that would never be. The sword of truth impaled her. She wanted to roar but the pain was too deep, ripping her heart in two. When her vision started to blur, she violently swiped at her eyes, refusing to cry over him anymore.

Suddenly, there was a commotion downstairs. Doors slamming and voices. She swore if they woke her son, she'd be furious. Determined to stop it, she burst from her room and raced down the stairs.

"You need to be…" her voice faltered. Before her stood Thomas and Father Charles from St. Mary's Cathedral. The priest held a bible in his hand and had a grin on his face.

"Good evening, ma'am."

Thomas raced to her, bending on his knee. "You are right. I've been an idiot. I tire of politics, of the bickering there, of the denial of laws and acts that'd make this country a true land of the free." He took her hand with a pleading look in his eyes. "And so caught up in trying to eliminate the sins of this country, I'm about to lose the only person I love. I'm so sorry for being an idiot, for not doing what is right. Young Thomas deserves a better father. God knows, he has the best mother. Please forgive me."

She snorted. "Thomas, you have aided me a lot over the last few years, and the one thing I learned is painfully clear." She cleared her throat, her shoulders steeling under the indignity he made her feel wrapped with anger. "Just like those runaways we help, their independence we strive for, I know I don't need you. I can live and breathe without someone using me for his own political advances. My son will soon learn how to stand on his own and not be forced to serve another, *that* I can promise you!"

The priest's lips curled up a bit in a smile she could see, before he stepped back as Thomas came between them, his face contorted with pain.

"Jaquita, please, I beg you, don't leave me. I have been a dunce, lagging in many ways, I assure you, so I beg your forgiveness." He took her hand and dropped to one knee once more, burying his head against the back of her taken hand.

Her heart was thudding loudly, and as hard as she tried to see him, her vision blurred.

"I love you Jaquita. I have from the moment I met you. Please say you'll marry me, right now."

A tear escaped. The sincerity of his tone struck her heart deeply, despite the anger that fought against it. She knew he cared for her. Had claimed love many times, but never begged her to marry him since that day he'd left Allison. But this time, he had a priest to make it official. Wiping her eyes with her free hand, she looked past him at the Father Charles who held his grin.

"Thomas, I just don't know."

"Jaquita, as God is my witness, I love you and I can't live without you," he proclaimed loudly, staring deeply into her eyes, clutching her hand painfully.

She glanced at the ceiling.

Thomas shot her a questioning glance.

"I'm looking for lightning bolts, the type God would rain down on you for lying." Even her conclusion made her want to laugh, though why she wasn't sure. "Seeing as there are none, and you look rather intense, I guess I must believe you."

Thomas gave her a tight lopsided grin. "So will you marry me, my love?"

Again, her whole world was turning upside down. She wanted to marry him. She loved him, but he also drove her crazy! Inhaling deeply, she paused and then gave him a quizzical look, her eyes starting to blur again.

"Don't we need witnesses?"

Clarence and Aunt Lila came out of the side rooms.

"We're here for you, Miss Jaquita," Clarence stated.

Aunt Lila looked at her and winked. "I told you to stay clear of those white boys, all mischief and such."

Jaquita laughed, wiping her weeping eyes. "That you did. I should've listened."

"I thank God you didn't!" Thomas picked her up and spun her around in his embrace. Slowly he lowered her, the smile gone and a concerned look in his eye. "Will you marry me? Right now?"

"Why?" Her stomach flipped between his sudden change and the uncertainty she couldn't stop.

"Because I love you," he whispered in her ear before he tugged on her earlobe.

"I love you," she whispered back. "And yes, I will marry you."

He grinned ear to ear. "Father, if you please!"

She giggled. "Good thing you finally woke up."

"I agree." He squeezed her.

"You won't be able to do that much longer."

He turned, a questioning glance on his face, and then it hit him. "When?"

"Late next summer, the midwife reckons."

"Huzzah!" he yelled, picked her up and spun her about the room.

"Put me down before I get sick!" she warned as bile started up her throat. It retreated when he put her down.

"I love you, Mrs. McHenry." He kissed her deeply, so much that she couldn't breathe but wouldn't move for any reason. Inside, her soul sang.

The priest rattled off the ceremony and they answered the vows, but Jaquita only heard his love and that was all she needed.

~THE END~

# AUTHOR'S NOTES

During the time of slavery and not long after, mixed relations were strongly frowned on and even outlawed in some states. In this story, Jaquita is referred to as a mulatto because her mother was a slave and her father a white man. Her children were then referred to as quadroon with one grandparent Black and rest 3 parts white, and the next with more white heritage were called octoroon. Yet, by any 19th century viewpoint, any portion of Black could make that person subject to slavery because of the African blood in them. The destruction of the peculiar institution was the only way to change this way of life and it was fought over for four years in the American Civil War.

The Abolitionist movement had been in existence in the US since the early 19th century and grew in numbers by the time the War broke out. The sins of slavery were argued over by most of the country, so why hadn't it abolished slavery? The problem was, there were multiple abolitionist groups and they fought amongst each other, over money, over if the freed slaves should be sent back to Africa or not and whether they should be given the right to vote, once they were freed. The last argument is what started the women's suffrage movement, as white men considered giving Black men the right to vote, but not white women. In the end, Black men did get the right to vote fifty years before women could.

There are multiple resources used for this book. A few listed would give the reader a taste for the peculiar institution and its meaning on Americans in the 19th century.

# *Bibliography*

*"The Plantation Mistress"* by Catherine Clinton

*"From Slavery to Freedom, A History of Negro Americans"* by John Hope Franklin & Alfred A. Moss, Jr.

*"Soul by Soul, Life Inside The Antebellum Slave Market"* by Walter Johnson

*"Black Slaveowners, Free Black Slave Masters in South Carolina, 1790-1860"* by Larry Koger
*"Without Consent Or Contract, The Rise and Fall of American Slavery"* by Robert William Fogel

*"Within the Plantation Household, Black and White Women of the Old South"* by Elizabeth Fox-Genovese

*"Masters of The Big House, Elite Slaveholders of the Mid-Nineteenth-Century South"* by William Kauffman Scarborough

*"The New York Abolitionists"* by Gerald Sorin

*"The Peculiar Institution, Slavery in the Ante-Bellum South"* by Kenneth M. Stampp

*"Harriet Jacobs, A Life, The Remarkable Adventures of the Woman Who Wrote 'Incidents of the Life of a Slave Girl'"* by Jean Fagan Yellin

# Also by Gina

### Hearts Touched By Fire
*The Wicked North*
*The Key to the South*
*Rags & Hope*
*The Better Angels*
*Authentic Storm*

### Stand Alone Titles
*Her Eternal Rogue*
*The Wicked Bargain*
*This Love of Mine*
*Great & Unfortunate Desires*
*A Merry Wicked Christmas*
*To Kiss A Lady*

### The Gladiator
(Ancient Rome series)
*Love & Vengeance (Book I)*
*Love & Lies (Book II)*

# ABOUT THE AUTHOR

A *USA Today* Bestselling author, Gina Danna was born in St. Louis, Missouri, and has spent the better part of her life reading. History has always been her love and she spent numerous hours devouring historical romance stories, always dreaming of writing one of her own. After years of writing historical academic papers to achieve her undergraduate and graduate degrees in History, and then for museum programs and exhibits, she found the time to write her own historical romantic fiction novels.

Now, under the supervision of her dogs, she writes amid a library of research books, with her only true break away is to spend time with her other life long dream – her Arabian horse – with him, her muse can play.

Made in the USA
Thornton, CO
05/03/22 20:37:07

148be0bd-4111-4cc3-83db-c8a969773060R01